A NOVEL

LEGACY

HUNT

EZEKIEL ELIZALDE

Elizalde Publishing

Published by Elizalde Publishing
Kyle, TX

Distributed by EZ Publishing

Design and composition by Neil Gonzalez
Cover design by Neil Gonzalez
Cover images used under license from ©adobestock

Print ISBN: 979-8-9856031-2-5

First Edition

Thank you to Mom and Dad for support and ideas for
biomes. Thank you to Renae for ideas of animals.
Thank you to Eddy for helping with the map.

AUTHOR'S DREAM

A gaping hole in the earth sits in front of us, filled with mysteries. The path leading inside is rickety and brittle, yet almost seems alive. Our guide takes us further into this cave that now opens up into a cavern. As we travel deeper, we see creatures that resemble bats but have a yellow tone to their body. They hang upside down on the ceiling towards the left of the path unbothered. Our guide gives us information about these creatures saying that when they scatter, any other organism that watches them will go blind. Now with our nerves on edge, we enter a crevasse or a ravine in the cavern with crystalized walls searching for some kind of treasure. Suddenly, a gargantuan monster enters from the darkness of the ravine with a long, round head and razor sharp teeth of a teal color. Its elephant-like legs shake the cavern until the beast falls on the ground and lies motionless. The beast seemed old and frail, like it was time for it to pass. Then we notice that the teeth were a treasure we've all been searching for. An impenetrable material that is said to be of myth. We take the teeth from the beast and the ground begins to rumble. Dirt falls from the ceiling and my partners are scrambling to get out of the ravine. The cave is collapsing and we do everything we can to climb or crawl out of this ravine. The area starts to fill with sand, causing the exit to shrink. All hope seemed to be lost until a small plane and my companion dragon flew through the cavern to pick us up. My dragon picks me up and my partners are picked up by the plane. We fly away from the ravine towards another exit while we dodge boulders and stalactites. The bat-like creatures begin to scatter, so I close my eyes in order to prevent myself from becoming blinded. My dragon takes me through the cave as fast as possible, maneuvering right, left, down and up again. Until finally we make it to the exit, where the rickety path was and the plane pushes through rubble while it's smoking. The light shines on us for our success in retrieving the treasure alive. Then the dream ended.

This story is based on that dream.

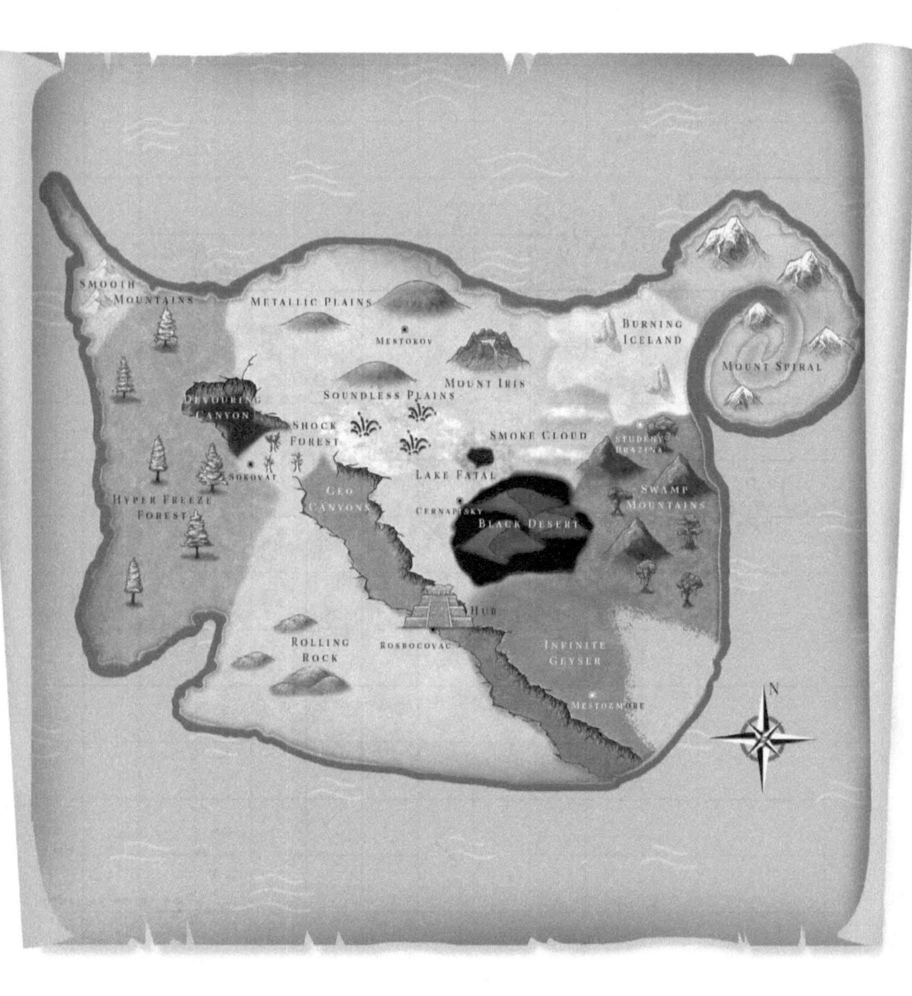

SMOOTH MOUNTAINS
METALLIC PLAINS
BURNING ICELAND
MESTOKOV
MOUNT SPIRAL
DEVOURING CANYON
MOUNT IRIS
SOUNDLESS PLAINS
SHOCK FOREST
SMOKE CLOUD
STUDENY BRAZINA
SOKOVAT
LAKE FATAL
SWAMP MOUNTAINS
HYPER FREEZE FOREST
GEO CANYONS
CERNAPISKY
BLACK DESERT
HUB
ROLLING ROCK
ROSBOCOVAC
INFINITE GEYSER
MESTOZMORE
N

1

THE DEVOURING CANYON

Light clouds hover over a dark and eerie canyon surrounded by forest to the left along with silver rock terrain to the right. The sound of large flapping wings comes from within the clouds as a black dragon soars the skies. Its head has four distinct dark horns, one on each side of the head, and a pointed face with razor sharp teeth. They have four legs, thick claws, and a tail much like a whale's.

Riding the magnificent beast is a young man named Elliott who is wearing padded armor lined with gadgets placed on his wrist, chest, and thighs. He wears a thin metal backpack and a mask that sticks to his chest when not put on. His short, brown hair waves in the wind as they fly closer towards the canyon that seems to have no bottom.

"Alright, Chernak! Are you ready for this next treasure?" Elliott asks his dragon companion.

Chernak shakes his head, seeming like he's saying, *I was born ready, you know that.*

Elliott pulls out a small, blue handheld device with a radar screen. The device, called a waypoint, has an arrow pointing towards the inside of the canyon that says 'Beating Pearl'. A treasure that is an orb that can power an entire city for years to come.

As the two of them go deeper into the canyon, the light slowly dwindles. Elliott takes off and reaches into his backpack to find a set of goggles where the lenses protrude outwards. He puts them on, flips a switch on the left side to the goggles, and the lenses shed bright light. Even the illuminating goggles are not enough to light up the ominous cave, but it allows Elliott to see in his close surroundings.

The sound of whistling, small flapping wings, clacking, and scratching against the walls echoes around the area. Even with the many times that Elliott has been in this canyon, it still sends a chill down his spine. The most valued treasures mainly linger in the darkness of these caverns, which makes it all the more dangerous to find them.

The waypoint emits a high pitched, repetitive beeping sound while Elliott and Chernak go deeper into the canyon. Elliott looks around with his goggles for any sign of light, ledge, or the treasure. Although, finding a treasure on the ledge would be too easy. Elliott knows better, as he has been on many journeys for extreme treasures in the past. At his young age he has become one of the greatest treasure hunters to exist. From his experience, he knows that this treasure will be a difficult but fun one to acquire.

The natural light from above dissipates so much that it looks like a distant star in the sky. Chernak growls and shakes his head, *How much further? This is getting lower than usual.*

Elliott observes the waypoint, "Not much further I don't think. You're fine though, you can see in this darkness. Why are you complaining?"

I'm not complaining, I'm merely asking a question.

"Eh, that sounded like a lot of whining coming from a big, strong, sand dragon to me," Elliott sasses.

Due to that remark, Chernak snorts and jerks his back up to lift Elliott up off his saddle a little. Elliott yelps as he grips the saddle tightly with his right hand and his goggles with his left to prevent them from falling off.

Yeah a big, strong, sand dragon that can just let you fall.

"Serpent's crystals! It was just a joke!" cursed Elliott. A common curse referring to glacier serpents that live in the Hyperfreeze Forest, a moist, forest terrain that quickly and dramatically changes into a frozen environment. The phrase emphasizes the waste that the serpents produce that look exactly like crystals.

Make a joke that's funny, then I'll laugh.

"Just keep going, you dirt dweller," Elliott said with frustration.

That's what I thought, Chernak seemed to say as he continued to look around the canyon.

Chernak's vision is keen, being able to see through any kind of darkness. Not only that but he has the capability to see through rock as it helps a sand dragon when hunting. They are adapted to dig at great speeds and he must be able to see when doing so.

The waypoint begins to beep faster and Elliott says, "Wait!" in order to stop Chernak from descending. The arrow on the blue screen pointed forward near the exact level they had stopped at. Chernak's wings continue to flap in order to tread in the air. The air around them was cold and damp with a feeling like the walls were caving in. The eerie sounds heard from before silenced, the only sound being the wings of Chernak and the beeping of the waypoint.

Chernak snarls, *There's a ledge and a hole in front of us.*

"That might be our way in. Can you land?" Elliott asked.

Chernak huffs and puffs like he is laughing, *Can I land? Of course I can.* He then shakes his tail up and down to move forward and plants his four feet onto the small, rocky ledge. Elliott swings his leg over to meet with his left and jumps off the back of his companion.

Gazing at the human-sized crack in the wall with the gleaming goggles, Elliott sees a faint, pulsing, pink light further inside the confined cave. Nothing else becomes visible to Elliott other than the rocks near his face and the light that dimly irradiates.

Elliott looks back up at Chernak, "I'm going in there. You stay put in case something goes wrong."

Chernak snorts, *Something always goes wrong. You of all people should know that.*

Elliott opens his mouth to talk but hesitates as he couldn't argue against it. In every hunt that the two of them venture on there is most certainly something that ends up going sideways. Of course, both of them have overcome them in the past. Countless hunts that have not only been inside the Devouring Canyon but in plenty of other places such as the Black Desert, the region that Chernak's species is from.

"Alright fine, you stay here 'until' something goes wrong, how's that?" Elliott emphasizes.

Chernak snaps his head to the side, *Just make it quick. I'm starving.*

Elliott tilts his head in indignation but says nothing against it as Chernak is always famished. He turns back towards the small crack in the wall and heaves himself into it. The claustrophobic crevasse almost encases Elliott with every inch of movement. His back, arms, and legs all scratch against the rocky surfaces. The armor and backpack protects him from any injury, although he can feel every part of it.

Chernak sits down in an exaggerated motion by slamming his body onto the ledge, pouting. He doesn't like doing nothing while his only friend strolls into a dark room full of who knows what.

Chernak growls, *Why couldn't I just dig in there?*

Elliott's goggles point back through the small opening, "Because you could collapse whatever is in here and maybe even awaken something that shouldn't be woken."

Chernak plants his head on the ground, *Whatever.*

Elliott chuckles, "You're so dramatic."

Chernak said nothing, or appeared to say nothing, and instead let out a low growl of anger.

Elliott continues, and as he moves further he hears the sound of running water echoing in the distance. The narrow passage finally opens up into a much more spacious room. Although, the walls seem to be darker somehow. The pink light is clearer, changing from a magenta to a neon pink as it pulsates.

Elliott stands up to get a clear view of the room. He peers closely at the darker walls to notice it isn't rock. It appears like fuzz with tiny specs of dust that scatter across it. It moves in a wave-like fashion all along the walls.

"Ah grappling moss, just as I suspected," Elliott says in a quieter tone so as to not disturb it. Grappling moss is a plant that is sensitive to loud sounds and high frequencies. If disturbed it will transfer itself onto the ground or lowest parts of a room and ensnare anything around it. The vegetation induces an acidic material that can eat away at rock when provoked.

Suddenly, Chernak from the other side of the wall stamps his feet. *What's taking so long? Are you dead yet?*

The moss begins to increase its wave movement. Elliott gasps and moves back to the narrow crack. "I will be dead if you don't stop making noise, you whining ox!"

Immediately Chernak ends his stamping and sits down again. *You take forever,* he seems to say.

The moss returns to normal by settling its waving motion. Elliott releases his breath as he didn't realize that he had been holding it. He wants to open his mouth to call back to Chernak but dismisses the choice. He knows that if he made too much noise it would provoke the moss.

Elliott continues through the hallway towards the ever increasingly illuminating light. The cave opens a bit more with the light shedding enough for Elliott to take off his goggles. This room is open and the ground in front of him is dry like a drought. As he steps into the room, the ground cracks beneath his foot. Elliott tenses, stopping his body from making any further motion. As soon as the thin rock stops cracking, he pulls his foot back onto the solid surface.

He observes the ground intensely, looking at all parts of the room. Every inch of it was covered in the thin ground he almost fell through. Knowing what was beneath the floor was impossible unless something or someone broke the surface completely. Elliott grabs a large rock from close by in order to check what is down there. He lifts the dense rock and launches it in an underhand motion in front of him.

The thin floor immediately shatters like glass, creating a massive hole in the earth. A couple seconds go by as Elliott waits to hear the rock bash into the ground below. The sound is faint, indicating that it's a far way down and that if Elliott had gone any further he would have for sure turned into a pancake.

Elliott looks up at the other side of the room. There is a patch of sturdy rock much like the surface he was standing on at the other side. However, it is a good ten, up to fifteen feet away. Making a running start to jump over the chasm wouldn't be much trouble. But Elliott has little room, the hallway is thin and behind that is the grappling moss.

Instead, Elliott has a plan. He never travels unprepared and always has something up his sleeve. He reaches to the underside of his metallic backpack to press a button. As soon as he does so, a light turns on at the top of his pack in the shape of a pentagon. The pentagon moves and a floating droid with white slits for eyes flies in front of Elliott. It makes a high zooming sound as it makes its way.

"Hey, Coil, I might need a little help here," Elliott asks.

Coil is his robot helper that Elliott made. A multi-tooled and curious little droid the size of his hand designed to provide with various ways of cutting, grabbing, or even showing the way to obtaining a treasure.

Coil, excited to help, scans the thin surface as if he read Elliott's mind. He floats around, searching for a solution. Coil then flies towards the hold made by the large rock, looks over at Elliott, and seems to cheer by giving a small jump in mid air.

"What are you trying to say?" Elliott asks.

Coil floats towards him again and stops. He turns back towards the hole to create an arch motion.

"You want me to jump on your head?" Elliott implies.

Coil nods several times and readies himself above the hole.

Elliott shrugs, "Alright, don't drop me."

Coil shakes as if saying that he would never do such a thing.

Elliott steps backward until his body is in the narrow hallway. Once he is ready, he bursts into as fast a run as he can. Once at the edge of the brittle surface, he pushes off to reach his next foot onto Coil. Just before Elliott lands on him, Coil pushes upwards to make the impact more stable. Elliott lands on Coil and pushes off to aim for the other side. His hands make it to the solid ground, his legs nearly miss as his right clips the edge and breaks some of it. Now Elliott begins to slip with his right foot dangling from the edge.

Coil, with no hesitation, reveals five wires for arms and grabs hold of Elliott to hoist him back up. Coil increases his thrusters upward as much as he can. Elliott strains to pull himself back up and brings his leg up to roll his entire body onto the ledge. Coil lets go, releasing what looks to be a sigh of relief. But no breath comes out as he is a robot.

Elliott inhales and exhales heavily, his heart beating out of his chest as he very well could have fallen. He looks at Coil, "Thanks, I don't know where I would be without you, buddy."

Coil makes a cheerful zooming noise again. He then flies towards the entrance to the next room where the sound of running water can be heard louder in this chamber. The light is brightest in the next room, creating sparkling shapes on the walls.

Elliott stands up to peer into the next room slowly as he doesn't want to be caught or trigger anything. This next chamber is filled with running water that makes a spring. Steam fills the air which makes it feel humid. In the center of the room is a small island, surrounded by a waterfall that rings around it. The neon pink and magenta color lights the entire room. It beams through the falls which create the various sparkling shapes by refracting through it.

Elliott gazes around the room looking for any sign of danger. He knows that a treasure this valuable cannot be as easy as jumping over a chasm and sneaking past moss. There have been far too many instances where an extreme treasure appeared easy but soon almost killed him. There is a trick to this, he knew.

He moves closer to the spring and the water specifically. There is something odd about the water. From a distance and if not paying attention it could pass as water. Although, it's gray and the steam is odd as well. The water would have to be near an extremely high temperature such as a volcanic area and they were miles from any.

"Coil, scan the water for me, will you?" Elliott asks, still gazing at the water, or what seemed to look like water.

A white light comes on from Coil's face that covers part of the spring next to Elliott's face. A screen turns on the top of Coil's pentagonal head showing the name "Poltonic Acid". A highly corrosive acid that is produced in large bubbles beneath the earth. Sometimes they pop and the acid eats away at most rock materials until it fades.

"There must be a huge bubble right above us, Coil," Elliott says.

Coil produces another zooming noise but at a lower tone this time like he was amazed.

"I don't suppose you have a way to make a bridge, do you?" Elliott asks rhetorically.

Coil shakes his body but then springs up like he has an idea. He ascends towards the ceiling and aims his face up. A small opening forms between his eyes and a rope shoots out to grapple the ceiling with a metal point. He then descends back towards Elliott for him to grasp the end of the rope.

"Good thinking. Now I think I might need an umbrella," Elliott says, indicating that he needs a way in the falls without him burning alive.

The opening between Coil's eyes closes and he happily glides towards the acidfall ring. The edges of him expand to make himself wider and he blocks the acid falling on one side to make an opening for Elliott to swing.

Coil is corrosive resistant, a feature that Elliott didn't want to miss when building him in order to prevent making repairs and reaching into difficult places like this one. The material comes from features of certain fish in Lake Fatal, a region on the continent that has a large and corrosive lake with marshy areas full of corrosive resistant organisms. Although Elliott's armor would be able to protect most of him, Coil cannot be damaged by any corrosive material.

Elliott puts on his mask that has been sitting on his chest and folds over his face, the top of his head, and the back. The helmet is made of a thermoplastic, specially made to be breathable, flexible, and durable. The respirator is in the shape of a triangle and the visors for the eyes are in X's that glow red.

The experienced treasure hunter tugs on the rope to be sure of its grip. Once satisfied, Elliott steps back to gain momentum and pushes off the ground, bringing his legs towards his chest. As he swings past the pool of acid, he releases his grip to land just under Coil to prevent himself from hitting his droid or the acidfalls.

The timing is perfect, Elliott lands with no extra force nor losing his footing. Now he has the full sight of the Beating Pearl. The pearl is sitting on a pedestal around three feet high. As it pulses, he can see the inside of the pearl which appears like a gaseous storm.

Elliott investigates around it, looking for any traps or anything that is out of the ordinary. The pedestal is lined with carvings creating columns, waves, and dots all around. Nothing seems to protrude. Nothing seems covered. Nothing seems ominous.

Elliott nods in satisfaction and pulls out an empty cloth bag from his pack. He reaches for the pearl, carefully placing his fingertips on the underside of the sphere. He feels the weight of the orb settling on his hands and lifts it off the pedestal. Elliott stares unmoving, waiting for something to happen. After a few seconds, Coil releases a cheerful zooming sound.

Elliott laughs nervously, "Well alright! Another treasure for our record." He then stuffs the pearl inside the cloth bag and places it into his backpack. Suddenly, the acid falls begin to strengthen and the spring starts to fill. Coil struggles to stay hovering to keep the acid from streaming in the one section.

"Uh oh," Elliott mutters. The spring quickly fills up and

Elliott calls to his droid companion, "Coil catch me!" and jumps without hesitation. Coil grabs hold of Elliott with his metal tentacles and uses every bit of his thrusters to pull Elliott up. The weight of the hunter is too much, causing them to descend. Elliott's feet nearly touch the spring and instead crash against the floor of the exit.

Coil lets go, looking like he's out of breath. Elliott staggers but catches himself against the wall. The corrosive liquid overflows, rising over the rocky surface, and flowing towards the rest of the rooms.

"Come on, Coil! The exciting part started!" Elliott says.

They both head for the exit back towards the thin rocks Elliott almost fell in. Without any hesitation, Elliott sprints and hauls himself across the chasm. However, his time in the air wasn't enough. His feet break through the slim floor but his arms are able to catch his weight on the more sturdy surface.

Elliott's heart is pounding, he holds his breath as he strains to hang on to the ledge with his legs dangling over the darkness below. Coil, with a worried zooming noise at a higher pitch, wraps his arms around Elliott once again to heave him back up.

The acid behind flows over into the chasm, burning through the dry rock. It seems like it wouldn't be able to reach them with the time that they have. But the rigid walls around them begin to crack and leak with the acidic material. As Elliott swings his body with the help of Coil back up, the walls burst with debris shooting past and near them.

"Thanks Coil! Now back into your pod! We're gonna catch our flight!" Elliott yells.

Coil obeys by planting himself back into the pentagonal indent in Elliott's backpack. Once Coil is secured, Elliott continues his run into the next room. He looks around for the grappling moss to realize that they have already made their way towards the floor.

It's too late to stop himself. Elliott is already launching himself into the moss, which reaches for him with large waves and vines. He puts his feet in the clearest spaces possible but still crushes the moss scaling the floor. He bobs and weaves around the dark vegetation. Some of which manage to grapple his arms and legs, burning the armor protecting his skin.

The acid fills the room even more quickly, consuming the provoked moss. Elliott tears through the burning plants restraining him to make his way towards the narrow passageway.

What's going in there? What did you do this time?! Chernak roars.

Elliott squeezes through the slits in the cave and yells, "Prepare to fly, Now!" ignoring the banter from his dragon companion.

Chernak obeys, leaps off the ledge hovering next to it, and waits for Elliott. Elliott is shoving his way through the small opening, almost touching the acid flowing behind him. Just before it splashes onto him, Elliott rolls out of the cave, quickly gets his feet under him, and hops onto Chernak's back.

The acid pours out of the narrow slit, creating an echoing roar across the canyon. It causes the previous noises of scratching and whistling to come back but at an extreme volume. The noises come from thousands upon thousands of winged creatures flying straight towards Elliott and Chernak. Chernak leans side to side attempting to avoid the incoming animals. However, it's impossible to avoid all of them as they smack Chernak under his stomach and his legs.

Chernak roars, not in pain as these creatures are smaller than him, but in anger as he hates being shoved and tossed around. He flails around trying to strike back at any of the mysterious creatures with his tail and wings. He is successful with many, but it isn't enough to get around and up safely. Chernak is becoming tired and he can't hold them off forever.

Elliott, desperately trying to avoid any contact, tries to think fast and can only come up with one solution. He leans into Chernak, "I think it's time to dig!" he says.

Chernak shakes his head in agreement and flaps his wings towards the side of the canyon. Elliott slides his feet into footholds on the sides of the saddle, making a *click* once installed. He presses his stomach against the saddle and Chernak's back, using Chernak's horned scales as cover.

Chernak gains speed, readies himself, and plunges into the rock on the side of the canyon. The sheer amount of force creates a hole in the shape of him. His wings slice through the earth as if it was paper. Debris flies across Chernak's four horned scales on his face much like a drill. His head, eyes, and mouth are all unphased by the amount of soil they are breaking through.

Elliott grips onto the saddle, waiting for them to be above the surface. If he raised his head at any point he would hit rocks, possibly flying backward if he's lucky or take his head off if he's unlucky. But he's used to this form of transportation as he and Chernak have done this plenty of times before.

Chernak continues to cut through the ground until he bursts out into the blinding daylight. He twirls in the air, shaking the excess debris off of himself. Once he becomes right-side up, Elliott straightens and lets out a triumphant, "WOOOOO!"

"That was thrilling!" Elliott screams.

Yeah, for you. Guess what? I got to sit there for most of the time. I didn't even get to watch you. Chernak snorts.

"Oh . . . well . . . you whine too much anyway," Elliott teases, as he takes off his mask.

Chernak growls, *Don't test me!*

Elliott laughs, "How about this? We'll get some nice grub once we get home. Your choice. How does that sound, buddy?"

Chernak lets loose a low grumble, *That sounds . . . fair.*

2

ROSBOCOVAC

Chernak soars through the air high in the sky, high enough to see various parts of the continent. As they fly south-east, to their left is a large portion of green. Nothing else, just tons and tons of grass that makes up the Soundless Plains. An eerie region that causes every creature to go deaf temporarily. Nothing can be heard in this area and nothing seems to live there either. Many treasure hunters have explored the plains before in search for legendary treasures, the hardest treasure there is, but all have failed. Either they give up looking or sometimes they go insane.

Past the Soundless Plains are the Metallic Plains. A vastly metal covered region created by the famous Mount Iris. A highly active volcano that constantly erupts with iridium. The iridium is used to make currency in the shape of small coins with the letter 'I' imprinted on it. That's exactly what people call their coins, I's. Named after the letter. The region is covered in iridium, coloring the ground in silver with hints of oily rainbow. The city of Mestokov was placed there years ago in order to mine the iridium. No one is allowed over there unless authorized to work. Otherwise, they are imprisoned and stripped of all their treasures. In the distance, Elliott can see the massive, violent volcano spewing out hot lava.

To Chernak and Elliott's right and behind is the Hyperfreeze forest. Further in front of them is the Rolling Rock. An interesting terrain full of various treasures but constantly turns like a giant wheel rolling towards the coast which is farther south. Every ten minutes the region rolls and reveals more treasure from beneath the earth. It rolls at a drastic rate, several meters at a time.

Right below them is the Shock Forest creating thunderous noises. One of the most dangerous terrains, the Shock Forest has what looks like dry and dead trees. However, each tree emits thousands of volts of electricity, creating a purple shock that flies upwards. As Elliott looks below, he can feel his hair stand up. The town of Sokovat will be built here as Elliott can see the construction going on next to the electrified forest.

Where they are heading back towards is the Geo Canyons. A dry and dusty terrain filled with small gems, crystals, and precious rocks. A gargantuan canyon cuts through the entire region like a giant scar. Most people live here where they have access to an abundance of treasures. Not only that, they are just next to the capital city of Rosbocovac.

Chernak glides Elliott straight towards the capital city. Most people call it the Hub, where they can receive waypoints to find treasures. The entire economy relies on treasure hunting as the continent is filled with them. Not just gold and jewels, but also relics, vegetation, sometimes animals. Whatever people sign up to obtain, they bring the treasure right back to the Hub where they get I's in exchange.

That's exactly what Elliott is intending to do once he turns in the Beating Pearl. Chernak comes closer to the large city of Rosbocovac. The largest buildings look much like temples and ziggurats. Built with crimson and yellow stone that shines in the sunlight. The whole city is suspended above the monstrous canyon, making it a bridge across it. The rest of the smaller buildings are rustic, metal, rectangular compartments for housing mainly. Some sit on the brick flooring that makes the bridge, others dangle below it by various bars and cables. Each side is protected by a gate with pillars that line rhythmically across the walls. The gate is almost always open. The only times it closes is in times of crisis like storms or even a herd of Oxenrock.

Thousands of people walk in and out of the city as Chernak lands safely with Elliott jumping off of the saddles. The middle temple-like structure towers above everything else. It is stacked layers upon layers of brick and rock. Surrounding it are four smaller ziggurat structures that still significantly stand taller than the rest.

"Home sweet home!" Elliott says as he pulls out the cloth bag holding the pearl.

Elliott walks through the gates, passing people around him that give him interesting glances with wide eyes, smirked faces, and jaw drops. People are either flabbergasted by the orb Elliott carries or the giant sand dragon that walks beside him. Elliott has lived here and turned in many treasures here for years yet people never cease to be amazed or terrified by the young hunter.

Along the streets are hundreds of people buying and selling food. Smoke fills the air around the suburban parts of the city followed by the smell of barbecue meats, steamed vegetables, and candied fruits under large pavilions and canopies. Among others, people sell clothing and jewelry that consists of beads, shells, gems, even bones.

Some people sit on boxes of various sizes gambling on a small table with dice, cards, and sticks. Grown men toss in their silver I's into the pile and complain about the result they get as the man across from them scoops their winnings into a bag laughing. Another man punches the other after losing their entire savings in a game of cards. The two of them sprawl around on the ground while everyone else either steps around them or watches with interest.

On top of a balcony towards Elliott's left is a couple holding hands in front of a pastor. The woman wears a big red wedding dress while the man wears a crimson tuxedo with a pink tie. The streets are too loud to hear but the couple eventually press their lips against each other.

"Of all the places to get married. Why here?" Elliott asks Chernak.

Chernak shrugs his large, black shoulders, *Guess they couldn't wait any longer.*

"No kidding," Elliott laughs.

The main temple building in the center of the city is where people go for their treasures. It's always crowded as people are always turning in and trying to obtain new treasures. All the money is stored here as well, which is why they call it the Bank. The Bank provides money based on what quality treasure a hunter turns in. A treasure is rated on a scale of Easy,

Mediocre, Hard, Extreme, and Legendary. Most people turn in Easy and Mediocre as they are the easiest to obtain with little risk factor.

Hard and Extreme treasures begin to threaten the lives of the hunters and are more difficult to find. Legendary treasures have never been found. They are the most difficult treasures to obtain either because they are hidden extremely well and/or hunters die every time they look for one. The Legendary treasures are what people attempt to find in order to be the first. That's what Elliott is hoping to accomplish.

For now, he has been searching for Extreme treasures, which is what the Beating Pearl is labeled as. Not many hunters are able to come back with such valuables, much less have obtained multiple. But Elliott is known for the one hunter to have gained the most Extreme treasures in hunter history. Now he plans to be the first to bring back a Legendary treasure.

As Elliott and Chernak walk closer towards the Bank, people begin to wave, giving their warm welcomes. Some step to the side giving disgusted looks with the corners of their lips raised. Some pat Elliott on the back congratulating him on another successful hunt, asking if he found the pearl. Of course, Elliott gladly says he has and shows them the illuminating bag.

The crowd in front of Elliott begins to disperse as a man with a massive stature steps in front of him, blocking his walkway. His hair is thick with dirt and dust followed by a scruffy beard. He wears a shirt that seems too small for him but obviously used to show off his pectorals. He rests his thumbs in his belt with a golden emblem of a crystal. His pants are baggy covered in pockets full of change. He is at least a head and a half taller than Elliott, looking over most of the people in the crowd.

Everyone quieted down once he began to talk in a deep voice, "Look who decided to come home. And with the pearl it looks like."

Elliott smiled up at him, "Yes I did, and I'll be getting my money now if you'll excuse me."

"Nah nah I'll take that right off your hands," the giant said.

Elliott raised an eyebrow, "You can't turn it in unless you have a waypoint with your name, everyone should know that."

"Oh yeah that's right. Let's see, you're coming with me and your money is mine," he said, his eyebrows narrowing.

Chernak growls but Elliott puts a hand in front of him, "Don't worry, I got this." Elliott keeps his grin on his face, "Yeah I don't think so. Those flabby muscles aren't scaring anyone, Gigantor."

Gigantor's face flushes with red as the crowd around them chuckles. "You think your buddy lizard will keep you safe, stump?"

Elliott laughs, "I hardly need anything to send you home crying to your mommy."

Gigantor scowled, "What are you gonna do?"

At that moment, Elliott clicks his heels together that activates rough spikes patterned on the bottom of the boots used for climbing steep mountains. He raises his right foot and smashes down onto Gigantor's toes. Crushing bones and sending searing pain throughout his foot, causing him to scream.

From his pack, Elliott quickly takes a collapsible rod from the side, extends it, swings around Gigantor, and chokes him with it. Elliott heaves the rod into Gigantor's throat, causing him to fall backward. His giant body sandwiches Elliott into the ground but he keeps pulling towards himself.

Gigantor does everything to try to get loose, but the pressure that Elliott enforces is too much.

"Now listen, you don't touch me nor do you talk to me ever again. In fact, don't talk about me or my dragon again. Do you understand me?" Elliott says.

Near blacking out, Gigantor nods faintly just wanting the whole situation to be over. Elliott recognizes and releases the rod from his neck, causing him to gasp for air. Gigantor coughs, holding his throat as if he needs to spit something out.

"Come on, Chernak. Money is waiting for us," Elliott says as he stands up.

And food. Chernak snorts.

Elliott sighs, "Yes, and food."

Gigantor weeps while he holds his broken toes but is then silenced as Chernak's tail wails against his head, knocking him out cold. The crowd watching them laughs and clears the walkway for Elliott and Chernak. As they continue, the street becomes more crowded with people having to squeeze by one another. Elliott stays near Chernak as people will most certainly go around the large sand dragon.

The Bank always looks bigger when up close. The massive temple building practically touches the clouds and shimmers in the evening light like a crimson beacon. Bodies of people spew in and out of the temple through a large opening that always ends up being slowed.

Elliott and Chernak push through into the opening which opens into a wide space with columns lining the outside parts of the room. Rows of people wait at windows on the left and right side where workers with plaid suits, purple ties made out of a shiny silk topped with spherical, black hats. Each worker is discussing a matter with a patron, handing bags of I's or receiving them for withdrawals and deposits.

The floor is covered with rough tile made from clay, mud, and brick making a mix of gold and red colors. The ceiling creates a cube around two stories high scattered with chandeliers surrounded by glowing, yellow stones.

Along the walls are pictures of hunters posing in various positions. Some had their legs propped up on a rock while looking in the distance, others had their arms crossed, some with multiple hunters with their arms around each other. Those are the most famous hunters who found the biggest treasures like Ana the Witch who seemed to have disappeared in the Devouring Canyon but was able to find the Magnetic Fountains. A pair of streams that seem to hover in the air and connect towards a pool. None were Legendary, but all were Extreme treasures. The group were in front of a lost temple in the Black Desert. The man on the rock found a rare animal called a Cheneria, a feline which had large tusks on the sides of its face, spiky fur, and three tails found in the Hyperfreeze Forest. The woman who is crossing her arms and stands with a serious expression on her face found an artifact with an ellipse head and long arms in the Smoke Cloud.

At the back end of the lobby is an enormous desk stretching almost the size of the whole room. On each side is a stairwell leading upwards. The wall behind the desk are five screens each with multiple lists of names for treasures. Each screen is labeled going in order from left to right, Easy, Mediocre, Hard, Extreme, and Legendary. Some names are highlighted in green with a letter A next to it indicating the treasure is available for hunting. Others, mainly on the hard and extreme lists, are highlighted in yellow with the letters CH that labels as 'Currently Hunting'. One of them being the Beating Pearl under the extreme list.

Everyone in the room begins to eye Elliott, stopping their conversations, deposits, and withdrawals. He stops walking as everyone now falls silent, seeming like they're waiting for something to happen. The younger hunter smiles, opens the cloth bag, reaches in to grab the pearl, and lifts up in the air for everyone to see. The entire first floor of the Bank roars and cheers in celebration, a tradition that has been going on for decades every time a hunter brings back an Extreme treasure.

Elliott smiles, nodding in satisfaction as he has done this before several times. The crowd makes a path for him to walk towards the desk while the cheers begin to die down. An older man waits for him dressed in the same uniform without the hat. He has a shaggy, black beard and very short hair on the top of his head. His brown eyes light up as he sees Elliott walking towards him. As he gets closer, the man opens his arms in welcome.

"Elliott! My friend! Another Extreme treasure for the book, aye!" he says in an accent that emphasizes the R heavily in a low tone.

"Hey Bohdan! Just can't get enough. It might be getting a little too easy," Elliott says.

They both laugh hysterically, "That's why I like you! We're ready for a picture, huh?"

Elliott shakes his head, "No not yet. I want to get a Legendary first."

"Ah but you've already got . . . um . . . ten? Is it ten now?" Bohdan asks, putting his finger on his chin.

"Seventeen now. I think that surpasses the record by a good eight or nine. But I don't want a picture until I have all of those under my belt with a Legendary."

"Ah, then I will praise you!" Bohdan bows. "Let me see that pearl, eh."

Elliott sets it onto the smooth desk, the pearl still beating like a heart with neon pink. Bohdan raises it to his eyes that reflect its colors, gasping at its beauty.

"Ahhhh . . . she's perrty! How much do you want my friend?"

Elliott raises his eyebrows, "How high can I go besides the fifty thousand that's listed?"

Bohdan looks at Elliott now, "For you?! I can give sixty! Since you came in such a short time."

"I'll take that any day!"

They both point at each other, laughing synchronously. "You wait here, my friend! I'll get you your money!" The shaggy man then opens the double doors in the back to search for Elliott's reward.

Chernak nudges his friend on the shoulder, *So where are we getting food?*

"I thought you were going to choose?"

I can't think of anything, I'm too hungry.

"Well, not anything upstairs. It's too expensive and doesn't fill you up. What about Zuzana's? She always makes good grub," Elliott says.

Chernak hops with his tongue sticking out, *I love her! Let's go now! Now!*

Elliott laughs, "Just wait a second, we need our I's first."

Just as he says that, Bohdan rolls out a wooden wagon

containing two large bags of coins. "Here you go, my friend! It appears we might be running out back there, huh?" He and Elliott laugh together at Bohdan's humor.

"Chernak, you wanna carry the I's?" Elliott asks.

Chernak grunts, *Do I have to do everything?*

"Oh come on. We're gonna get food and then after that you can get some treats back at home."

His dragon seems to purse his lips, thinking about the benefits. The downside being to only carry the money back home. He not only receives food, but he gets a treat, too. Chernak then nods in satisfaction as the benefits outweigh the cons.

"You know I appreciate you, buddy," Elliott says.

Shut up. Give me those bags. Chernak seems to say.

His friend chuckles as he ties two ropes together connected to the bags that will hang on the saddle. He raises the rope for Chernak to put his head under and pick up the bags. To Elliott, the bags are unbelievably heavy, but for a large sand dragon it doesn't seem like a problem.

Elliott looks back at the shaggy man, "I might just be ready for a Legendary."

But Bohdan's smile quickly turned upside down, "My friend . . . uh . . . I like you. Truly I do. But . . . no one has come back from that. You know? I don't want to lose you, huh?"

"Don't worry, Bohdan. I'll be just fine," he says, still smiling. "I got Chernak with me along with Coil to help me. I'll come back in two days for that Colossal Tooth."

One of the listed Legendary treasures that is offering one of the higher rewards is the Colossal Tooth. No one really knows from what kind of animal or even if the animal is alive. However, it is supposed to be made of the most impenetrable material in the world. If used correctly it could be made into armor, weapons, tools, and more. Bringing back any Legendary treasure will definitely make history, but one that is more valuable might get more praise.

Bohdan looks up at the screen, then back at Elliott, and his smile reforms, "Ah I am confident in you! You come back and I will give you all the tools you need, huh?"

"I knew you'd believe! Just make sure you have enough money when I get back," Elliott laughs, making it contagious as Bohdan joins in hysterically.

They wave each other goodbye and the hunter and his dragon head out of the Bank. The sky becomes dimmer with orange as it turns to dusk. The streets continue to be crowded with activity but begin to fade as some pavilions for shops close up. Elliott leads towards the left side of the Bank towards a massive market area.

Hardly any buildings occupy this district. Mainly consisting of more canopies set up to cover the owners selling more home-made barbeques, knitting, jewelry, and knick knacks. The air is covered with smoke and steam from the grills beneath most of the unorganized canopies. It smells of fried fish, grilled meats, cooked bugs covered in sweet and spicy sauces that burn the nostrils, even sharks that are encased in candied sap.

This part of the city generally stays the warmest from all the cooking, almost like creating its own atmosphere. Elliott unzips his jacket to release some insulation. The sizzling of grease becomes deafening as they walk further into the congregation of canopies. Signs made of wood hang by ropes on different pavilions for names of the shops.

On one of the signs is the name 'Zuzana's' carved into it and highlighted with green and red paint. A foul odor spews out from inside the restaurant mixed with red meats. Tables and benches made of wood are scoured around in an unorganized fashion. In the back there is a massive grill that smokes with all kinds of food cooking. Hanging above are large bags that drip with orange sap.

On her cutting board next to the grill is a short old woman with brown skin, wearing a dirty blue apron and a wide brim with a towering centered hat. She held a large cleaver in one hand and a spatula in the other. Ferociously she chops a Glacier Snake, an ice blue colored snake with thorns that look like icicles on the head. She cleaves in multiple pieces with amazing speed and throws in on the grill, creating a sizzle.

Zuzana looks up to see Elliott and Chernak walk under the pavilion and she bursts into an excited yell with open arms, still holding her tools.

"My boys! My boys!" She laughs going for a hug towards Elliott as he stays cautious of the cleaver.

"Hi Zuzana! Something stinks in here, it smells good!" he says.

"Oh you! That means it's ready." She turns to Chernak, "Oh come here my darling!" and she wraps her small arms around his head. She tilts it to her level to give him several kisses which he seems to enjoy. "How was your trip? You didn't do anything too dangerous, did you?"

Elliott can't hold back his smile, "I . . . may have had some close calls."

Zuzana gasps, "Aye! You need to be careful!"

"It's alright, I'm always careful . . . sometimes."

The old woman chuckles, "Oh you! What can I get for you, my sweet saps?"

He looks at his friend, raising his eyebrows asking what he wants. Chernak points his head towards the menu board which hangs above the grill.

Get the giant glacier serpent!

"He wants a giant glacier serpent. I'll get one, too," he says.

Make it two for me! I'm starving!

Elliott sighs, "Make it two for him. So three total."

With sap!

Elliott purses his lips, trying to hold back any kind of frustration. "With sap, please," he manages to say calmly.

"Of course, my dears. Coming right up!" and she hurries to the grill to prevent any of her food from burning.

Once Zuzana gets to her grill Elliott darts his eyes at Chernak, "Seriously, anything else or forever hold your peace."

His dragon tilts his head as if he's thinking. *Well now that you mentioned it-*

"Don't answer that."

Chernak huffs and puffs to laugh.

The two of them sit down at one of the benches, Chernak lies next to it as he cannot fit. He puts his head onto the bench, letting out a big sigh. Elliott, now feeling the exhaustion from the trip and sympathy for his friend, reaches over to pet his dragon on his head and scale.

"Don't worry, buddy. We'll be home soon and we can rest. Then later we'll go for that legendary treasure."

Do you really think that we'll be able to find it? Chernak groans.

"I know we can," he says.

But there have been so many that have tried.

"I know. But they haven't had as much experience as us. Trust me we'll be the first. Some went to hunt without a plan and tried going into the Soundless Plains. We won't go for that. We're going to find the first legendary treasure and we're going to have the biggest party and praise Poclad has ever known. The whole continent. Think about it. Unlimited treats!"

Chernak thought, and as he had the vision with piles upon piles of treats he couldn't help but smile. But what made him even happier was imagining himself with Elliott next to those piles. As much as they tease each other, not a day goes by where Chernak doesn't want to experience an adventure with his pal.

Looking back at the grill to see where their food is at, Elliott notices a girl sitting closer towards the back. She wears a purple long sleeve shirt with the sleeves rolled up her forearms, utility belt with a knife, and dark green cargo pants. She has wavy dark hair and brown skin. One glance and Elliott's eyes sparkled with his jaw dropping at someone he thought was the most beautiful person in Poclad.

She is eating scorobeetles on a stick, a bug that has a large stinger hiding under the wings down the middle, blue skin, with horns at the top of its head and bottom of the chin. Most people would skip eating the stinger which she seemed to leave behind so far. It's an acquired taste as it is used in most liquors.

Chernak notices his friend hasn't turned back around in a few seconds. He lifts his head to see who he is staring at and can't help but grin. He nudges Elliott with his nose.

Stop drooling and go talk to her.

"Pfft, I'm not drooling! I'm just . . . just . . . " Elliott studders.

Oh, the high and mighty hunter can conquer any treasure but he can't talk to one pretty girl. How pitiful could you get?

Elliott's cheeks blush beet red, "I can talk to her! It's not any harder than finding a gemstone in the canyon."

Chernak spat, *Oh yeah? Go up to her. Right now! I dare you!*

His friend couldn't help it, and Chernak knew that. When Elliott is being challenged, he can't help himself but to accept it. This situation is no exception.

He raised his eyebrows, "Alright! I think I will! Look, I'm getting up and going over there now!"

Chernak laughs, *I would wish you luck, but it'll be more fun just to see what happens.*

Squinting his eyes in annoyance, Elliott turns to walk over to the pretty woman while his heart begins to beat faster. Butterflies flutter in his stomach the closer he gets. Usually he would be a fairly social person, talking to the managers, to random people if they asked what he was up to. But in this time trying to talk to someone he finds attractive is a whole new experience.

Elliott stopped a few feet away from her, still having her back turned towards him. He opens his mouth to talk but nothing comes out. No words are made to form sentences, the mind is absolutely blank. If he says the wrong thing she might hate him, or think of him creepy, or weird.

Chernak, still waiting for Elliott to make a move, becomes impatient. He stealthily slithers his tail past the other benches and chairs towards his friend. Before Elliott could say anything, he was shoved forward right next to her, crashing against the counter.

The girl jumps as she wasn't expecting someone to be slamming their body into the furniture next to her. He glares at Chernak with furocity and the dragon can't help but laugh hysterically.

The beautiful girl chuckled, "Are you alright?"

Elliott blushed, his face turning bright red, "Ye-Yeah I'm fine. You'll have to excuse my friend. He can be a little irritating," he says as he glares at Chernak again in the last sentence.

She peers at the laughing sand dragon and then back at Elliott, "Wait, you're Elliott, right? The famous young hunter that everyone talks about?"

His eyebrows and the corner of his lip rise. "As a matter of fact I am." He sits down on the bench next to her. "I've acquired seventeen Extreme level treasures, the most famous one being the Forgotten Tombstone. My most recent was the Beating Pearl that I just turned in," he bragged.

The Forgotten Tombstone was a treasure in the Smooth Mountains where a tombstone lay on the side of one of the mountains. Buried beneath it was a sarcophagus that was empty but had markings of an ancient language. The tombstone had a name but was never deciphered.

"Interesting," she said, leaning on her hand and seeming intrigued in his resume.

"I didn't catch your name, by the way."

"I'm Eva, extreme treasure hunter. I've got a few treasures under my belt, too. One of them being the Shell Model," Eva said.

The Shell Model was an extreme treasure that was an empty,

fossilized shell that contained a model of a city made of rock. It was perfectly intact and was used as a blueprint to make the city of Cernapisky in the Black Desert.

"That was you? That find was amazing! I always admired that discovery!" Elliott praised.

Now it was Eva's turn to start blushing. She smiles as she turns to take a drink from her wooden cup. "Are you planning to go look for a Legendary?" she asks.

"As a matter of fact, I am. I'm planning to be the first one to find one and bring it back," he says with full confidence.

Eva turns back to him, "My crew and I are planning to look for one, too. Looks like I have some competition."

"Indeed you do. But in the meantime, may I buy you a drink to toast to your next hunt?" Elliott says.

Her eyes squint while she smiles at him, thinking about the offer after she is about to finish eating. Her lower lip protrudes outwards and she nods, "I think I'll drink to that. I'll have to take it to go though."

"Excuse me, Zuzana!" he says. Immediately she turns towards him. "Could I get a Shell Shock, please?"

One of the more fancier drinks, Shell Shock is made with saliva from a venomous and poisonous animal called a cephoshell. A cephalopod with a round shell, pointed head, and five tentacles. The saliva is carefully boiled and brewed into the alcohol to make a hard taste with bittersweet, smelling sour and fishy.

Eva raises her eyebrows and nods, "How generous of you. Maybe next time I can buy both of us drinks when I have time."

"Next time?" Elliott asks, his face blushing again.

She reaches into her pocket to pull out a small notebook and pencil. Then she scribbles something in fast hand, but pretty handwriting, tears it out, and hands it to Elliott. On the paper reads *7.052.022 Mere Mansion,* with the first number indicating the district, the next three telling the street, and the last three showing which building.

"You should come by sometime. Then we can get something stronger," she said. Then Eva plucks the stinger off of the scorobeetle and puts it in her mouth, creating a soft crunch as she chews. Her eyes are a beautiful hazel, Elliott recognizes as they continue to peer at him with attentiveness.

Elliott, filled with a racing heartbeat and twitterpated by Eva's flabbergasting glow, is at a loss for words. No sentences seem to form except for the sounds, "Uh," or, "Um."

She giggles and says, "I'll see you later, alright?"

"Uhh . . . oh yeah! I'll uh . . . see you at this place," Elliott scrambles to say while gesturing at the piece of parchment given to him. She waves goodbye and walks out of the pavilion.

As he watches her walk out, Elliott then realizes that his food just came out to their bench. The steaming hot glacier serpents have a nice golden brown color to its icicle-like skin, taking away its natural ice blue color. Its fangs have been plucked from its pointed head. Three of them are wrapped around a large stick about a meter in size each dripping in an amber sap. Chernak looks at each one of them with a watery mouth and he licks his lips as he leans closer towards them.

"Hey!" Elliott screams just before Chernak could take a bite, "You better not eat my food!"

Chernak stops, darting his eyes at his best friend that seems to say, *I wasn't going to. What made you think that?*

"The way you looked at it, dummy. Who's drooling now?"

Chernak ignores the comment so that he can concentrate on eating. Elliott sits down to begin feasting on the delicious food before them. Both of them lick the sap from one middle portion of the snake and bite into the meat. The sap makes their mouths salivate, it has a sweet and buttery taste with a hint of acidity. The meat is only complimented by the syrup, containing tender, juicy flavor. It's cooked perfectly with the meat peeling right off the stick.

Chernak looks like he almost eats the stick along with the serpent in seconds. He quickly moves onto the second one as Elliott still works on his, only about halfway through. Although, Chernak does have a much bigger stomach than Elliott does.

"So who's the pretty lady, my sweet sap?" Zuzana asks suddenly, causing Elliott to jump while having food in his mouth.

He swallows and says, "She's . . . she's a hunter, I just met her."

"Oooo she's pretty, dear! I bet you two would make a wonderful couple!"

Elliott blushes in embarrassment, "I wouldn't know, I haven't exactly gotten to know her very well."

"Oh, I know a good couple when I see one. You remind me of my husband and I when we met in Mestozmore. We danced and watched the fish make beautiful colored shapes. He told me I was more beautiful than the water colors," Zuzana says, sighing just by thinking about it with a huge smile.

"I didn't know you were married. That's a nice story," Elliott says.

"I was, he was a sweet man. Just like you, my sweet sap," she said, grabbing his cheek.

Elliott laughs, "Thank you, Zuzana. That really means a

lot," and he reaches for a warm hug that Zuzana graciously accepts.

Chernak makes a groan saying, *What about me?* Obviously Elliott understands him, but Zuzana seems like she can read his mind too when she responds by saying, "Oh you too, my sweety!" Then she proceeds to give him a hug that he leans into.

As Zuzana pulls away, Chernak glances at the rest of Elliott's food, basically saying, *Are you going to eat that?* Elliott, who knows that he's full but still has a sense of annoyance since he bought that serpent for himself, reluctantly passes the food over to his friend with a long sigh. Before he knew it, Chernak slurps up the serpent as if someone was going to take it from him.

The young hunter stands up and says, "We should be going home now, Zuzana. It's been a long day, but a good one."

"Of course, sweety! Go get some rest! Don't forget to give this one a treat," she says, pointing at Chernak who looks to be smiling at the comment.

"Oh I think he's had enough treats these past few days," Elliott says and Chernak gazes at him bitterly.

"One treat won't hurt him. Be careful now, my sweet saps!" she says, waving goodbye.

"We will," Elliott responds and waves back as they walk out of the restaurant while Chernak picks up their money and follows close behind.

The streets are significantly less crowded as the night falls upon them. Countless lanterns are now enlightened, hanging from various buildings, pavilions, and light poles. Some stores are still working, many of them being bars or small canopies for gambling. The Bank is the brightest of all, illuminating the inner parts of the city with the brick that it is structured with. It glows crimson red mixed with a dusty gold.

Elliott and Chernak head towards a massive staircase leading downwards below the city. This is the Low district where most housing lies. Large boxes made of metal hang by long and thick beams connected to the floors of the main city. Bridges made of the same material connect to all of the suspended houses. Below is a huge drop going to the bottom of the canyon where there is a river flowing, sparkling gems on the sides, and dry brush cascading throughout the natural formation.

The two of them walk down the bridges, past a few homes, towards the outer part of the district to a slightly larger metal, rectangular house with a smaller dwelling protruding to the left. The entrance door is an ellipse shape that shows a vault handle with an indention of a hand in the middle. Above it is the peep hole that cannot be peered in from the outside. Not a single window is a part of this side of the dwelling to prevent people from looking inside.

Elliott places his right hand into the center of the handle, pressing it further inwards to allow the scanner on the inside recognize his fingerprints and hand shape. The handle clanks, indicating the door unlocking, and Elliott turns the handle counter clockwise to open it. Chernak climbs on top of the dwelling to the other side where the balcony is while Elliott enters through the door.

Inside is a spacious home where each corner has a different significance. To the immediate right is the kitchen where there are two large burners with a cone shaped top. Metal cabinets on the top hold most pots, pans, plates, and bowls. The bottom holds utensils and cleaning supplies that haven't been touched for a while. Two long, vertical handles indicate the food storage when pulled out, with the top being the dry products and the bottom being refrigerated.

The next right corner contains a workbench and counter filled with various parts, tools, and broken apart gadgets. Wrenches, blow torches, glass containers with bubbling liquids of all colors. An empty armor stand sits close by it.

To the left is a hammock in the corner next to the balcony hanging above a large, rectangular, black sand pit for Chernak to sleep since it is close to his natural environment. The corner next to the entrance is a separate room for the bathroom. A small area that has a sink, toilet, and tub but compact.

Another vault door sits on the left wall for all the storage of money and trophies from the treasures that Elliott has acquired. Some are portions of the treasures he found as he has the option of keeping some of the treasure if it can be shared or take the money and a picture in the Bank.

The balcony is closed off with a wide double sliding door that can be opened with a green button to the right next to the armor stand. Elliott goes to press it, allowing Chernak to walk in and lie down in the sand pit. There he slides head first and rolls around, kicking up some sand onto the floor. Elliott doesn't care much since it's his normal routine.

Then after taking off his backpack, Elliott presses the button to release Coil again so that he may roam around and charge on a small plate connected to a cord leading to a purple generator half the size of the pack. The little bot floats around joyously going towards his charging plate. He lies onto the plate where the rim glows blue.

Elliott unzips his jacket and armor to sit on the armor stand where he notices scorch marks and tears in the shoulder padding. Probably from the grappling moss or the acid, he thinks. Normally he would get to work repairing the damages, but the day has been long enough that Elliott wants to settle down and rest. His shoulders slouch, feeling the dreariness throughout his body.

Coil's robotic eyes look over at his master and he floats towards him. He makes a gesture pointing towards the damage with a high pitched, questionable tone seeming like he's asking if he should fix it.

Elliott laughs under his breath, "No that's alright, buddy. I'll fix it tomorrow. You did great by the way, I couldn't have done that trip without you," he says, feeling like he hasn't appreciated his mechanical companion enough.

Coil happily leans towards Elliott where he pets his head and Coil hovers back to his charging plate. Now that his eyes become droopy and his walk begins to sway, Elliott heads towards his hammock above the sand pit. He pulls the straps on his boots open, slips them off along with his socks, and walks into the sand pit. The soft sensation of the sediments relaxes his muscles. Lying on the hammock only adds to the comfort of it all.

Elliott releases a long sigh of exhaustion. As he closes his eyes he says, "Goodnight, guys."

Chernak expresses the same energy with a low huff in response and Coil powers down.

3

THE CREW

Two days have passed since Elliott acquired the Beating Pearl. In those days, he had time to rest and prepare for his next hunt, that being the legendary treasure, the Colossal Tooth. He has repaired the damage done to the shoulder pad with simple sewing and fusing. The rest of the days consisted of relaxation, wandering around the city, and the usual bickering between him and Chernak.

With all his tools and supplies packed in his backpack, his padded armor jacket fixed, Elliott is now ready to set off on his next journey. First he heads towards the Bank to receive his waypoint. The morning rises, making the sky illuminate brighter with orange ever so slowly. The traffic in the streets begins to increase in activity as Elliott and Chernak walk into the Bank.

Half of the workers sit at their booths while others start trickling in late, some scrambling to put on their plaid jackets.

Bohdan at the front desk dusts the area with a circular, fabric duster. While wiping an area of the desk that causes him to cough, he notices his favorite patrons walking towards him.

He smiles graciously with open arms, "My friends! Back already, are we?"

"Oh yeah we are! I think today's the day, I think it's time. Let me take the Colossal Tooth!" Elliott says eagerly.

Then his eagerness quickly turned to concern as Bohdan's smile diminished to a frown. "Listen . . . my friend, you know I love you and I love what you do for my business–"

"Bohdan, what are you saying?" Elliott says now furrowing his eyebrows.

"Someone has already claimed the waypoint today," Bohdan says.

Annoyed and angry now, Elliott sighs trying to contain his frustration. He's prepared for the past two days expecting to pick up the waypoint. Not only that, but it has been the treasure he's been eyeing for months, gaining experience for. The Colossal Tooth is the most valuable treasure listed in the Legendary category, so of course he's going for it. Up until now, the treasure was never picked up by anyone in his time as a hunter. Now that he's ready to go, someone has taken it.

"I've been looking at that treasure, Bohdan. You know that," Elliott says as calmly as possible.

In a surrendering gesture, Bohdan replies, "I am sorry, my friend. But you also know it's first come first serve. I do not take reservations."

Elliott does know that, which is why he can't say anything against it. "Who claimed it, may I ask?"

"It was a woman, very pretty in fact. Her name was . . .

hmm uh, Eva! That was her name!" Bohdan says with a snap of his fingers, proud of himself for remembering.

Of course, Elliott thinks. The worst thing is that if she took the waypoint today, that means she probably already headed out. If she did, there was no chance of talking to her about a compromise. But he did still have the address, so he can still go towards it and possibly make a deal about the treasure.

"If I may, my friend," Bohdan proposes, "There are still treasures available for use. I have the Glacier Emblem, a risky and cold one. I have the Light Consumer, I know you're familiar with the Devouring Canyon. There's also the Stellar Staff, I believe those could be to your liking."

Elliott waves hand in a dismissive gesture, "That's alright, Bohdan. I'm sorry I got a little angry, I'll figure out something else. Thank you."

Bohdan's smile swiftly returns, "Of course, my friend! If you want the treasure so badly, you could ask to join them!"

While looking at the address that Eva gave him, he reluctantly thinks about the idea. "We'll see, thank you again."

"Anytime, my friend!"

Elliott walks out of the Bank irately with Chernak close behind who rotates his head seeming like he's saying, *So what now? Do you want me to eat her?*

His two-legged friend gives him a questionable look, "No, we're going to talk to her. We've prepared for too long for that treasure."

What if she doesn't come back with the treasure? Everyone gives up or doesn't come back anyway. Couldn't we just wait?

"I'm not waiting that long, we've waited long enough. Plus there is a chance she could find it and bring it back, she's a good hunter, I know it," he then releases Coil out of his pack. "Hey, buddy. Can you lead us to this address?"

Coil faces the piece of parchment with a green light scanning it. Elliott could just follow the street signs since he knows the city fairly well. But some avenues can be closed off, too much traffic, or he could even just make a wrong turn. Coil will make sure they go down the quickest route as he has a map and status of the city. The little droid begs them to follow him to the right of the Bank.

District seven out of twelve is a more wealthy part of town. Most buildings are touching one another in large rows. Some are malls, high quality restaurants, and mansions. It is much smaller than the lower district which is labeled as district zero.

There is much less activity here as there are minimal pavilions and canopies set up. The only reason they would set up here is to possibly have a small barbecue for a celebration. These streets are considered the cleaner parts of the city because everyone who lives here tends to work indoors or prefers to stay in their prestigious home.

The color of each building looks brand new, the morning light reflecting off of them. Houses with pointed roofs, symmetrical build, and elegant stature are the most notable parts of the district. Rhombus shaped windows decorate each building, complimenting each trapezoidal topped door.

The most distinguishing mansion that Coil leads the others to is a three story building with circular, star shaped windows and a large dome at the top. The coating around the mansion is a rusty, yellow and red paint. The entrance is a large set of double doors similar to all the others.

Immediately, Elliott knocks on the front door impatiently. A couple seconds go by until someone from the other end begins to unlock and open the door, that person was Eva. Her eyes sparkle and she puts on a surprised but happy smile on her face.

"Hi there! It's been a second, also a little early, don't you think?" she says.

But Elliott wasn't amused, he's still thinking about the waypoint she supposedly has. "I'm not here for a drink. I heard you claimed the Colossal Tooth waypoint," he said.

Her smile begins to dial down, "Oh . . . yes I did. What? Were you wanting it?"

"Actually, that's exactly what I wanted," he said, a little hopeful.

But his hopes were quickly destroyed as she said, "I'm sorry. But my crew and I were also planning on it. Plus it's first come first serve."

Yeah I know that, Elliott thought. "How much would you want for it? I can pay any amount," he said.

But Eva was already shaking her head, her smile gone completely, "It's not for sale. We're going on this trip for the adventure and the title, not the money."

Elliott scoffs in frustration. There seemed to be no way to receive this waypoint. Maybe this isn't worth it, he thought. Like Bohdan said, there's plenty of other Legendary treasures to go about. So there is a possibility that he can find any of those.

Almost giving up hope, Elliott says, "Is there any kind of compromise we can come to?"

Eva's eyes narrow and she tilts her head while she thinks for a couple seconds. "You could come with us," she says, which is exactly what Elliott was afraid of.

Working with others has never been something that Elliott considered in the past. It has always been Chernak and Coil, a unique set for him that he doesn't want to change. He always had his own way of hunting without dealing with the responsibility of other people. Then he would have to worry about their own style of hunting.

"I'll say this," Eva says, bringing Elliott's attention to her, "We can do a bet. You come with us and the first person to physically touch the treasure gets sixty percent of the profit and the title."

Now there was something interesting for him. He would have to suffer the consequences of being with other people, but would still be able to be named a Legend Hunter. He could care less about the money since he has plenty back in his vault. The title is what he wants.

Elliott sighs, "Deal. And this is temporary. I don't normally work with others."

"That's fine, you might like them. You never know," she says, opening the door wider for him and Chernak. For Chernak though, she opens the both doors for him to fit.

The parlor they stand in is open with rustic patterns on the floor made of tile depicting the nearby land. A set of stairs lead up and to the right directly in front of them. A cylindrical chandelier hangs in the middle of the room that lights most of the area. To the right looks like a study, where bookshelves line the walls. Four cushioned chairs sit in a circle with a coffee table in the center.

The left room has two large, gold colored couches facing each other. On the wall is a pentagonal fireplace with a metal gate protecting it. The floor here is covered in red, soft carpet.

Towards the back a kitchen and dining area can be seen. Several used pots and pans sit in the sink and on top of the stove. On the countertops are numerous kinds of plants blooming with berries. Yellow pods, maroon half-spheres, and teal petals. The dining area is just one large, wooden table with six chairs pulled up.

What grabs the attention of both Elliott and Eva is the sound of sawing, clashing, screaming, and laughing. Words are being said but they can't make out what they are saying.

"What in Heied's mane is going on up there?" Eva curses, referring to a green, lion-like deity in the Soundless Plains.

Are you sure we should've agreed to this? It sounds like someone is dying up there. Chernak snorts.

"You know, I'm wondering the same thing now that I think about it," Elliott responds.

A puzzled look falls on Eva's face, "Are you talking to me?"

Elliott, now realizing that he was talking to his friend sand dragon in front of someone else, says, "Oh sorry, was talking to him." He jerks his thumb towards Chernak.

Eva still doesn't quite understand, "You're saying that thing can talk?"

"In a manner of speaking. He understands everything we say and makes whiny sounds when he responds," he mocks.

Hey! Chernak growls.

"Don't even act like you don't complain, because you do," Elliott says to Chernak, who falls silent.

Eva shrugs her shoulders but now wonders if Elliott is serious or not. By the looks of it, Chernak did seem to respond like a person. She does know that stranger things have happened in this world. With that in mind, she almost forgot about the noises happening upstairs and gestures to Elliott to follow her.

The second floor is more confined but starts with an open room with a large screen connected to multiple controllers by wires. The controllers are octagonal prisms with a joystick at the top and the wire on the bottom. Two shelves sit side by side of the screen with circular cases that hold cartridges for games and films.

The rest of the floor is one long hallway spreading from left to right. Each side has three sets of doors, the first two being bedrooms and the one at the end a bathroom. To the left of the main room is a ladder leading up through an open, square hatch. The sound of arguing becomes louder, coming from the third floor.

Chernak takes one look at the hatch and shakes his head. *Yeah I'll just wait here,* he says.

"Sounds like you need to lay off the treats," Elliott laughs.

Chernak growls but knows that he shouldn't say anything back fearing that Elliott will have something better to say.

Eva and Elliott climb up the ladder into a massive floor. The left side is an organized set of shelves and desks with baskets full of metal materials and parts. Giant power tools lie around the table such as saws, drills, even washers. Gears are piled on top of each other like a cassette hanging on a stand.

Next to the workbench is a cartography table with a map of the entire land on a billboard. A line stretches from the city of Rosbocovac in the middle of the Geo Canyons, going towards a point to the right at the Infinite Geyser, a region that is covered entirely of water. Then it points a little northwest towards the Black Desert, then further to the left again making a zigzag to the Burning Iceland, and finally ending into Mount Spiral.

A mountain range that creates a spiral at the corner of the continent.

The most distinguishing feature in this entire floor is the tall pedestal with a clamp on the top holding an airplane. It is rugged but still a magnificent piece of work. The coating was a dark turquoise, the propeller hangs slightly loose, and with three passenger windows on each side. The landing gear are floats to skid across water with wheels hiding underneath.

Elliott's jaw dropped at the sight of it, amazed that someone actually had one. In the continent of Poclad, vehicles such as planes are incredibly hard to come by. No one sells them because of a law to limit the amount of environmental destruction. However, if one were to only land in cities or flat areas with minimal or no habitats and have a permit, they are allowed to fly it.

After staring at the rugged but beautiful plane, Elliott can't help but notice the hysterical, spiky haired man in the cockpit. He seems to be laughing at the woman yelling at him from below with curly blond and red hair tied up in a ponytail. She wears a utility jacket with several wrenches and cargo pants. Next to her is a bald man wearing a green collared long sleeve who looks like he's just enjoying the show. All of them looked about the same age as Elliott, early twenties.

"What are you scrap runners doing?!" Eva yells.

Every one of them jumps at the sound of her voice, sharp and agitated. The first one to speak is the other girl who points at the one in the plane.

"Radek is screwing with the engine while I'm trying to make repairs!" she says.

"I'm not screwing with it," the spiky haired one called Radek says, "I was helping with the process," he laughs.

"You're literally holding onto the throttle!!" she screams.

"Radek, get down here right now," Eva says.

The bald one chuckles as he turns to look at the newcomer in the room. "Who's he?" he asks.

Elliott, still staring at the plane, doesn't hear the question directed at him. He continues to be flabbergasted at the magnificence of the vehicle. He doesn't notice the question, but he does notice Eva introducing him to her crewmates.

"This is Elliott, he's going to help us with the hunt," she says. Eva looks to make sure her guest is paying attention. Satisfied that he's listening, she points to her crew, "This is the Mere crew. Marketa is our mechanic and engineer, which is why one would get angry when another messes with their work."

"Damn right!" Marketa says.

"The one in the plane is Radek, he's our pilot," she continues. At that moment, Radek struggles to get down from the plane, eventually slipping and falling to the ground with a thud. She sighs in an irksome manner, "Unfortunately, he's our only pilot."

That didn't sound appealing, Elliott thinks.

"And that's Evzen," she points at the bald one. "He's our biologist and cartographer." He waves an awkward hello.

"Wait," Marketa says, "Is he 'the' extreme treasure hunter? The one with a sand dragon? The one with the most treasures in history?"

Elliott blushes, he's used to people cheering every time he brings back a treasure but has never spoken to a fan, ironically.

He subconsciously scratches the back of his head, "Yeah that's me."

"Are you going to be a member of our crew?" Evzen asks eagerly.

Elliott's smile faded, "I'm just here for the one trip."

His eagerness dilated as quick as it came, turning into disappointment. Aw damn, Elliott thought. He didn't mean to hurt his feelings.

"Hey, but . . . I'm looking forward to working with you all. I think it'll be fun," Elliott reassures, doing his best to fix his mistake.

That seems to do the trick as Evzen's face lights up again with excitement. Before anyone could say anything else, Radek pops up behind Evzen with a look in his eyes that seems a step above excitement. Something a bit scary to Elliott as he can't tell what it is. Joy, delirium, neither words seemed to fit. The best word he could connect to this guy's green and blue eyes was crazy.

"Do you want to see the plane?" Radek says with the widest grin on his face.

"Oh well, yeah. How did you–" Elliott couldn't get anything further as Radek snatched his hand, pulling him towards the plane.

"Her name is Fiala! And she is the prettiest soul in the universe!" he says.

"Don't forget who built her," Marketa added.

Elliott turned to her, "You built this?"

"Her!" Radek corrects. Marketa pursed her lips at the comment.

"It took a few years but she's made from scraps that we bought as we collected I's from previous hunts. Putting it together was the easy part, just some blowtorches to fuse it together, bolts and screws. The engine was the hardest part, but it runs on steam and electricity, that's the troubling part," Marketa explains.

"Why is that?" Elliott asks.

"Most of the time we've been using fire ice to power it, and the next cycle of it doesn't come into stock for another month and we ran out."

Fire ice is the most common fuel source for the continent. It comes from the Burning Iceland where a type of heated ice block that produces heavy amounts of steam. The ice melts very slowly in a process called sublimation, a transition from solid to gas. It is mined under the surface where it is condensed and heated to create these blocks.

"But you said it can run on electricity, can't you charge it?" Elliott wondered.

"We can, but the amount of electricity to power it would only be able to take us to one city and back. Then we would have to constantly charge it with a generator but we don't have that kind of power," she says.

"What about shock root?" Elliott suggests. A type of vegetation grown in the Shock Forest where the trees emit massive lightning bolts into the air.

Marketa thinks for a second and shrugs her shoulders. "I can install a shock root, but no one is able to obtain that unless you're head of the Bank. They're not in stock yet, they're still building the complex."

"It wouldn't hurt to go over there and ask," Elliott says confidently. "Chernak and I can make the trip up there and back in a day's time."

"Who's Chernak?" Evzen asks.

Elliott smiles, "You like animals, right? You're the biologist?" Evzen nods and Elliott continues, "You're in for a treat."

He beckons everyone to come downstairs, where Chernak lies waiting patiently at the bottom of the stairs. His head shoots up at the sound of everyone walking down the stairs. Seeing three unknown people, Chernak stands up.

Who are these idiots? He seems to say.

"This is Eva's crew. We're going to help them," Elliott says.

This is too many people. Chernak snorts.

"I don't like it as much as you but–" Elliott was cut off by Evzen squeezing between them.

"Oh what a magnificent beast! You are so utterly beautiful!" he says.

Chernak backs away a couple paces, surprised by the suddenness of the man in the sleeveless utility jacket.

"Please, oh mighty sand dragon, may I feel your scales?" Evzen begs.

Mighty, huh? The dragon steps forward to let Evzen observe more closely.

He peers at the helmet of Chernak in complete happiness. Elliott raises his eyebrows and looks to Eva, wondering if this is what he always does.

Eva shrugs, "You get used to it. It's not every day he gets to see a sand dragon. Much less a friendly one."

"You are just the most handsome creature I've ever laid eyes on!" Evzen goes on saying.

Handsome? Chernak says grinning.

"Don't let it get to your head," Elliott mentions.

As Evzen gets a feel for Chernak's neck, he quickly finds out that Chernak likes being scratched under the horns. This causes his back leg to kick with pleasure.

"So buddy, we need to go to Shock Forest to pick up a root. You up for it?" Elliott asks.

Yeah yeah, sure. Just . . . a bit longer. Chernak says as he continues to enjoy excessive scratching coming from Evzen.

Once finished, Evzen turns to Elliott, "Oh can I go with you? I've always wanted to ride one!"

Elliott hesitates, he was planning on going by himself quickly with little distraction. At the same time, he doesn't want to disappoint him again after what he said earlier about the one trip. Elliott looks at Eva, who doesn't need words to ask for Evzen to go. She gives a head tilt and lets her lower lip out in a begging manner.

He sighs heavily, "If it's alright with Chernak, then yes."

Chernak takes one look at the young bald man staring at his own eyes and gives a nod. *He seems alright to me.*

"Yes! I'll get my gear!" Evzen screams and sprints up the stairs.

Radek seems to be trying to match the stature of Chernak. "You seem pretty tough. What do you got?" He attempts to push over the dragon, who effortlessly pushes him back with his leg.

"You idiot, the tip of his tail probably has more muscle than you," Marketa says.

As Elliott begins to walk out the door, Eva hands him a small bag that jingles with coins. "Here's some money for the root," she says.

"Don't worry about it, I'll pay for it," Elliott responds.

"You shouldn't have to, please I–" Eva was cut off.

"No, it's alright. I insist. Consider it payment for your troubles," he says.

Eva smirks, slightly surprised by the kind gesture, "Thanks," is all she could mutter.

As everyone stands outside, Evzen sprints right back out the door with his leather pack. He stands beside Chernak, trying to figure out the way on top of the saddle. Elliott assists him in the foot straps and hoists him up.

"Be quick, no detours. And please take care of him," Eva says to Elliott.

"Don't worry, it'll be like my casual extractions," he says and sits up in front of Evzen. "Hold onto something," he tells Evzen who immediately grabs his waist.

Elliott pats Chernak on the back, telling him he's ready, and they lift off the ground. Evzen's cheer progressively fades as they drift away from the city.

4

THE SHOCK ROOT HARVEST

Chernak glides into the canyon heading northwest. Tons of small birds can be seen at the bottom where they hide in the dry vegetation. The rock on the walls of the canyon glistens rusted gold and red with hints of silver. The canyon leads directly towards the Shock Forest.

Ever since they left the city, which was just a couple minutes, Evzen cannot help but feel exasperated about the ride.

"This is absolutely phenomenal! You are truly the greatest creature alive!" he screams.

Chernak lets a grin loose. *Oh I'll show you phenomenal.*

"Please don't," Elliott says, but it's already too late.

His companion tosses and turns to show off to his new friend. He gains momentum to make a large loop facing upside down. Quickly he brings them closer to the walls where they can grasp a better look at the minerals. He faces them parallel to the ground, tip toeing on the rocky surface. The entire way, Evzen is cheering with delight.

Elliott, who would normally enjoy these rides, feels a bit more cautious now that they have an extra. "You should probably take it easy, buddy. You might piss off some bird," he warns.

What bird is going to be that big of a problem? Chernak says arrogantly.

At that moment, the sound of another pair of wings flapping comes from behind them. They are heavy and powerful flaps that can carry something much larger.

Elliott and Evzen look behind them and both their jaws drop along with their hearts. "Well I'll be, that's a studded raven," Evzen says.

The creature is about twice the size of Chernak. The feathers seem like they're infused like studded leather armor and have about the same color, brown with bronze spots. The beak is the most terrifying part as it is long and sharp. It releases a shriek that echoes through the canyon.

"He doesn't look happy!" Elliott says.

"She, actually. You can tell by the lighter color. You're right in saying she's not happy, you can tell by the back of her head that the feathers are standing up," Evzen explains.

"No time for a lecture! Chernak, step on it!" Elliott says urgently.

Chernak doesn't hesitate to obey. He flaps his wings harder to pick up speed but the raven is already catching up quickly. The acceleration seems to be a little too quick to notice as the pointed beak snaps at them, nearly catching his tail. Chernak's heart skips a beat, causing him to pick up the pace as much more as he can muster.

The raven goes for another snap that strikes just under Chernak. Just before he thinks he's in the clear, the raven swings her head up, colliding with Chernak's stomach. The impact lifts both Elliott and Evzen off the saddle, but Evzen flies completely off. Elliott stays on as he is clipped into the foot straps and he reaches as far as he can to catch his foot. Evzen screams in terror as he watches the raven trying to snatch her lunch.

Now about to lose his cargo, Chernak flies close to the wall to make the raven strike the wall. Sure enough, the sharp beak creates a gaping hole in the canyon, unphased by the impact. Dodging the attack causes Chernak to spin, making it harder for Elliott to keep his grasp on Evzen's boot. The spin nearly has Evzen graze his nose against the rock.

"Hold on!" Elliott manages to scream under the piercing pain from the strained muscles and tendons.

"You're the one holding on!" Evzen screams back.

"I'm telling myself that!" Elliott answers.

Before they know it, Chernak is knocked again to the side by the dangerous beak, causing Elliott to lose the grip of Evzen's boot. Chernak steadies himself and Elliott's heart stops. He frantically looks behind, below, left, and right. There is no sign of the fallen biologist anywhere.

That didn't just happen, he thinks. He had one job to do and that was to keep Evzen safe. Now he's no longer in the saddle with nowhere to be found. Then Elliott hears more cheering coming from his right.

"I'm the first to ride a raven!" Evzen screams.

Relief washes over Elliott that Evzen is still alive. Then a quick wave of dismay overpowers it.

"Serpent's crystals," Elliott curses.

The giant, armored bird notices the pest on her back and plans to exterminate it by shaking up and down, shrieking with anger. Standing up in his saddle, Elliott urges Chernak closer towards the furious bird. Elliott pulls a small lever on the top of his right wrist that clicks, preparing to fire a projectile. He aims just in front of the raven and several fireworks shoot out. They explode exactly where he wanted it, causing the beast to be confused and dazed.

"Evzen! Jump! Now!" Elliott screams, giving a helping hand.

Struggling to keep his balance, Evzen gets one leg under him and pushes off the massive wing. The two of them lock hands, pulling Evzen into the front of the saddle.

The studded raven, now livid, charges at Chernak, who can feel her presence gaining. Chernak cranks it up a notch to prevent himself and his companions from becoming her breakfast. He bobs and weaves, attempting to throw off the bird's maneuvers. It hardly seems to work as she is still dangerously close behind them.

"Alright, Evzen. I know you know quite a bit about animals. What can we do about that one to make her lose interest?" Elliott asks.

"She will definitely chase us until she catches us," Evzen says.

Elliott groans, "Great, anything helpful?"

"She will, however, not be able to go through tight spaces," he follows up.

Kinda figured, Elliott thinks. One problem is that there are no tight spaces as the canyon is enormously wide. The solution that Elliott comes to is having Chernak drill through the canyon wall. The next problem that arises is that he has never drilled with two people on Chernak's saddle. That can lead to a higher possibility that they will get stoned by the debris. Although, it seems like the only solution to get out of this situation.

"Alright, buddy! Get ready to drill! Go towards the right wall!" Elliott tells Chernak. "Keep your face as close to the saddle as possible, Evzen! And don't get up until we're back above the surface!"

Evzen doesn't hesitate to obey. As he does so, Elliott takes the mask from his chestplate and latches it onto his face and over his head, locking in place. He puts his face as close to Evzen's back as possible. Once he is ready, he urges Chernak towards the right side of the wall. Cherank gets one burst of speed, plowing into the rubble.

The raven, confused on what her soon to be food is doing, goes for another snap of the beak. Thinking she has them, she strikes the sudden hole in the wall, catching nothing but rubble and dirt in her mouth.

Elliott grips the sides of the saddle to hold himself down. But it doesn't prepare him for the large rock that bludgeons him in the forehead of the mask. The collision is strong enough to knock Elliott backwards with a grunt of pain, leaving him hanging by just the foot straps. After the first hit, several more projectiles pelt Elliott in the mask, the chest armor, and the arms.

The dig seems to take many minutes with endless crashes against the sediments. Finally, Chernak bursts out of the ground, countless meters away from the canyon. Once again, the dragon is soaring in the air at a comfortable pace.

Evzen rises in his seat, "Woooo! That was incredible!" he screams.

Elliott on the other hand, strains and struggles to sit up in his saddle. The damage done to the mask consists of various cracks and small sparks. The padded armor contains dents followed by streaks of dirt. His body from the waist and up aches. Every movement feels like a bone might snap. The injury to the head makes the world seem fuzzy.

Elliott slowly unlocks the mask from the back of the head and pries it off due to the damage. His head is bleeding just above his left eyebrow. His vision begins to readjust while a high pitched ringing in his ear becomes louder. Like a wave the volume rises and then falls, his senses come back to the wind in his face and the noise of Evzen cheering.

Evzen turns back to Elliott and flinches, "What happened to you?"

The injured hunter gives Evzen an angry look, squinting his eyes.

Evzen throws his hands up in a surrendering gesture, "Sorry I asked."

"Let's just get to the forest," Elliott says, still grunting in pain.

In the distance is the deadly shock forest. The trees seem desolate, almost dead. No leaves on the branches but grow as tall as most of the tall buildings in Rosbocovac. The soil around the terrain is rustic, like a drought. To the left of all the trees is the progress of constructing a new town. The walls protecting the construction are completed with fantastic masonry. Clean gray brick, straightened and even leveled with scorch marks on the side next to the forest. All due to the electricity emitted by the trees.

The only odd part that is on Elliott's mind is the forest seems dormant. No electricity comes from any of the dry plants. The only activity occurring is the construction of the buildings within the walls. Small cranes, inclines used to lift large bricks to pile on top of each other to create the outer coat of the scaffolding.

"That's weird," Elliott says as they come over the forest.

"What's wrong," Evzen wonders.

Elliott looks at his watch to monitor the time which is right at noon. "The forest should be erupting right about now."

After finishing his sentence, sparks of purple electricity fly out of each of the branches. Several bolts of lightning burst from the ground and into the air far past the height Chernak is flying. One of them erupts just in front of the dragon, nearly hitting them.

Chernak leans left to dodge it, almost hitting another lightning strike as they become more frequent. The sound from the thunder makes the air deafening. Elliott screams at Chernak to head for the ground but he doesn't hear a thing. Instead he urges him down towards the protected structures by tugging on the saddle.

The ride is a rough one, taking evasive action every second of the way. The bursts of energy become more intense the closer they get to the ground. Eventually, they exit the forest and almost crash landing at the entrance of the walls.

Elliott releases his breath as he didn't realize that he held it on the way down. Evzen jumps off the saddle, ecstatic about the entire ride. He even gives Chernak a few rubs over the horns.

The surges of energy continue to explode, mainly upwards but some straggling sparks make their way towards the walls. The trio heads for the gate to take shelter, but they begin to close. Their jog becomes a run, making their way safely into the inside of the complex.

The inside consists of workers in red, scaly suits while they carefully put together every building block. The suits are designed for protection against any electrical strike, making it a highly poor conductor. One of the workers stops his work, stomping his way towards Elliott and the rest.

"What the hell are you iry ants doing in here? No one is allowed inside the walls, especially during a surge!" the worker says angrily, calling them by a species of bug that lives in the Metallic Plains near Mount Iris.

"Pardon us, sir. But we came all this way in hopes that we may be able to pay for a shock root very quickly," Evzen appeals.

But the angry worker immediately shakes his head. "No shock root available," he says, his anger slowly subsiding. "We will sell once we harvest it and sent to the Hub."

"We're willing to pay more than the usual. If we could speak to your director maybe we can come up with an agreement," Elliott chimes in.

"You're speaking to him and the name is Ondra. I don't care how many I's you have. They could be bars for all I care. No one is receiving any shock root until the next batch has been sent to the capitol. Now, if you'll excuse me, I have a job to do. I suggest you wait until the surge ends for you to leave," Ondra says and walks away.

A wave of anger flows through Elliott's body. Making one

quick trip to get there is no problem. Even being denied the shock root wouldn't be too much to handle normally. But the trouble that they went through and the injuries that Elliott received is enough to almost make his blood boil. However, he's able to control his actions, preventing them from making any sort of mistake.

"Don't worry," Evzen says. "We'll find another way."

"What other way is there?" Elliott says, fists whitened. "Other than stealing the batch that they have, how are we supposed to get around this problem? If it was just me and Chernak, it probably would've been a smoother trip."

Evzen's eyes slowly look down in a depressed and guilty manner. His optimism slowly begins to weaken after Elliott's outburst. Elliott, now realizing what he said, sighs in regret.

"Evzen, I'm sorry. I'm just frustrated. Obviously the hit to the head doesn't help," he says. "I'm just not used to this, that's all."

"It's ok. I didn't mean to be such a burden," Evzen says, rubbing his head unconsciously.

"No, you're not a burden. You've been a great help with the raven back there. Look, you're right. There must be something else that we can do," Elliott says, trying to cheer him up.

It seems to be successful as a smile begins to form on the bald man's face, "We could harvest it ourselves!"

Blank faced, Elliott takes a few seconds to register what he said. In avoiding hurting his feelings again, Elliott says, "Alright . . . " holding back the rest of his frustration. "How do we do that?"

"Well, we need some protection, about half a foot long glass container, and some clippers," he lists.

Now Elliott's confidence rises again. "That doesn't seem too bad," he says, pressing the button on the side to activate Coil. The little robot hovers in front of him, prepared to do what he asks. "Hey, buddy. Could you grab some clippers from the pack and start crafting a half foot glass container?" Elliott asks.

With a joyful zooming noise, Coil digs into the pack to pull out a pair of large, sharp, single handed clippers. Then, at the top of Coil's head are blue sparks that begin printing a container. All of this while the surge continues outside.

"What about protection? Like the suits they're wearing," Evzen asks, gesturing at the workers' scaly jackets, pants, and masks.

"We'll have to make do with what we have."

"But that isn't enough. You need suits like theirs if you're dealing with shock root, you can get seriously injured," Evzen says in a worried tone.

"As if I'm not seriously injured already," Elliott says, caressing his possibly concussed head now covered with dry blood. "Plus, I'm not stealing their suits, I have morals, too. We'll just have to be extra careful."

Evzen grits his teeth just thinking about the possibilities that could happen. The biggest one being the possibility of electrocution from any of the trees they encounter. The reason why it is so dangerous is because of how easy it is to set off a surge. One wrong touch of the branch, one wrong step on the root could start an electrical surge.

While Evzen contemplates the idea, the surge begins to subside until the thunder is no longer heard. Though they didn't realize the sound of the electricity affected them so much, everything seems still. A very subtle ringing occurs in Elliott's ear. He beckons Evzen, Chernak, and Coil towards the exit.

Elliott waves goodbye saying, "Thank you for your time, Director Ondra."

Ondra scoffs and waves his hand in a shooing gesture while looking over blueprints.

Elliott shrugs, leaping on the saddle of Chernak and assisting Evzen up behind him. Coil falls right behind them as they take off away from the construction site, following the edge of the forest. The soil of the Shock Forest bleeds into the Geo Canyons in similar colors. Sediments of gold, bits of red, and a background color of peach. To the north is the infamous Devouring Canyon with the Metallic Plains and Hyperfreeze Forest adjacent to it. The silver, oily colored plains to the right and the thick glacier freeze forest to the left of it.

They travel until the complex is nearly out of sight towards the southernmost side of the forest. They land just outside the edge, being cautious about not disturbing any of the trees.

"Fantastic, now let's just get that one," Evzen says, pointing at the nearest tree. "We take a root and be on our way," he says with a slightly nervous tone.

"Will that work out for us?" Elliott asks.

Evzen tilts his head slightly showing his confusion.

"I mean is there a difference between harvesting a root from the edge versus more towards the center?" Elliott elaborates.

"Um . . . " Evzen seems almost afraid to say it. "There is, the further towards the center you go the more power it'll have. But it's really risky."

"Oh come on!" Elliott says in an encouraging gesture. "We're treasure hunters! All we do is take risks. You're going to tell me that even though you agreed to take on a legendary treasure you're nervous about taking a bit of shock root?"

Evzen wants to say something back, but in all fairness he knows Elliott is right. He starts running through the benefits and risks. The benefits are having a much more high powered root to take the plane further across the continent. Taking a root from the edge would still be beneficial, but it wouldn't take them as far and they would be able to have some power left over. The risk, however, is the high possibility that they will get electrocuted. Elliott might be fine with the padded armor he wears, but Evzen wears none. Then again, Evzen has gone almost every hunt with the crew without armor and they have been in several situations where he probably should've been wearing some.

While Evzen calculates every possibility and thought into his mind, Elliott begins walking into the forest. Before it's too late to notice, Evzen wakes up from his train of thought and rushes to catch up with his partner. The trees stand taller than what they seem from above. Each one towers from around ten feet to as tall as forty. Each one is separated from each other by at least ten paces, almost like they are repelling. The ground is loose rock, every step emits a crunch or cracking sound.

As they travel deeper into the static wood, Elliott's hair frizzles ever so slightly. The feeling of energy tickles the skin like something is about to pop. With all the sensations reeling, so does Evzen's nerves as he carefully watches his every step.

"That looks like a good one!" Elliott says suddenly, looking at a tree significantly wider than any of the others. He looks back at Evzen, "What do we do from here?"

The young biologist, now starting to sweat, reluctantly says,

"First you have to dig for the root, but be very careful about it."

Coil, hearing what he said, reveals four small mechanical shovels to break open the ground. He scoops in all directions to make a clean hole directly towards the closest root. Once Coil finds it, he pulls away waiting for new instructions.

"Now clean the loose dirt so you can make a clean cut," Evzen instructs.

Elliott, after putting gloves on, swipes, scoops, and picks away the gravel. Now the wrinkled, dry root is shown. The root is around six inches in diameter and who knows how long, white in color and full of creases. As Elliott cleans the rock away, tiny sparks form on the root, but not strong enough to make a large jolt.

He considers putting his mask back on, instinctively grabbing it but realizes how damaged it is. Now the nerves are getting to Elliott, knowing that he doesn't have the correct protection, much less a mask.

Elliott swallows nervously, "Alright, what now?"

With his heart beating rapidly and his breathing becoming more frequent, Evzen hesitantly says, "Well . . . now you need to cut."

Elliott readies his clippers in hand, "Where do I cut?"

"It's . . . not that easy. Just be super, undoubtedly, enormously careful," Evzen says, emphasizing each word with his hands.

"Alright," he says, frustration building up again. "But how do I know what not to cut?"

"It's invisible, that's why they use goggles to tell when a small jolt happens through the xylem," Evzen explains.

Elliott sits in silence for a couple seconds staring at the root, contemplating on what he just heard. "So you're deciding to tell me this now?" he says, gritting his teeth.

Evzen puts his arms in an 'oh well' gesture, "Positive that you can do it."

Now the nerves are off the charts for Elliott as sweat trickles down his cheek. He considers asking Coil where the best place to cut would be. But that plan is useless because he wasn't designed that specifically as there was never a need to. He sets the blades of the clippers hovering over the exposed root. As he does so, Evzen makes a physical reaction to flinch and place his hands over his mouth.

I'm just going to have to guess, Elliott thinks. "Serpent's crystals," he curses. There seems to be no other way. He considers pulling back but shakes the thought away. His heart beats faster, he can even feel it rising in his throat. Before he can think about anything else, Elliott pushes on the handles of the clippers as hard as he can. The blades slice through the root in one clean motion, causing a snap of the root.

Both of them jump, expecting for something to happen. Possibly a spark to fly, a surge to engulf them, but there was nothing. Absolute silence with a slight noise of the breeze from afar. Elliott chuckles with a crack in his voice and immediately cuts the other end of the root to pull out a piece of it about five inches in length. Once removed, he places it inside the glass container Coil made and seals it. The two of them relaxed their shoulders as they didn't realize how tense they made themselves.

Elliott waves the harvested root in the air smiling. "That wasn't so bad! What were we afraid of?"

A few seconds after he finishes his rhetorical question, the sound of crackling gradually becomes louder.

"Oh I spoke too soon, didn't I?" Elliott says in a defeated tone.

Bursts of purple electricity appear from the nearby trees, quickly dispersing towards the further parts of the forest. Evzen stands there in utter astonishment until Elliott snatches his arm, forcing him and Coil to sprint back towards Chernak. The roaring thunder is unbelievably loud, causing both Elliott and Evzen to hear a piercing ringing. Every step they take they nearly escape a bolt, zooming by their faces.

Finally, Elliott feels a burn followed by a severe tingling sensation coming from his left arm. A bolt had struck his hand, flowing through his arm. The impact nearly causes him to fall over.

Before they know it, they reach the edge of the forest, practically diving away from the surge once they are within a safe distance. Elliott sprawls on the ground flat on his back, waiting for the pain to subside.

As soon as it leaves, the two of them sit up and look at each other. Evzen can't help but point at the top of Elliott's head and let out an enormous amount of laughter. The hair on top of his head is sticking up perfectly straight from the amount of static electricity they came in contact with.

Evzen's laugh is contagious, causing Elliott to burst out laughing as well while he touches his own hair. "I bet you wish this happened to you too," Elliott says without thinking.

Both of them stop laughing, staring at each other while they take in the comment. Then, as fast as the laughing stopped, they began once again more hysterically than before. Chernak stares at them with puzzlement.

What got into you guys?

5

THE VODA SVELTO FESTIVAL

Eva paces around the suspended plane that Radek calls Fiala. Since the morning, Eva has been anxiously waiting for Elliott and Evzen to return with the shock root. Although, she is less concerned about the shock root and more concerned about them returning in one piece. What if they got lost? What if they got hurt? What if they died? All of these questions flew into Eva's mind.

While Eva is nervously walking, Marketa and Radek sit together shoulder to shoulder playing with a piece of crumpled paper. They attempt to bounce the paper with their hands to keep it from hitting the ground, passing it back and forth. The game doesn't last long as Marketa misses the hit, causing the piece to plummet towards her thigh and onto the floor. At that point she gives up and chuckles.

"What are you going to do with the prize money?" she asks Radek.

Radek scrunches his face and rubs his chin with his finger while he thinks about it. "I think I'd buy you a gift," he says.

Stunned by the response, Marketa blushes, not expecting him to give that answer. "Really?" she asks.

"Yeah, some new parts to upgrade Fiala," he adds.

Her soft smile quickly turns into a frown. The immediate response from Radek is a giddy smile followed by laughter. Marketa can't help but succumb to his contagious humor and chuckles with him.

Eva grunts as she stops her pace to turn towards the other two. "Shouldn't they be back by now? It's been six hours," she says.

Marketa takes a look at her watch, "Probably soon. The Shock Forest isn't very close."

"I bet they got hungry and ate the shock root!" Radek says with a huge smile.

Marketa and Eva stare at him with much bewilderment. Then again, they should be used to the extreme comments of Radek since they practically shape his personality.

Eva shakes her head as his insane comment gives her an idea. "Are you two hungry? I can make something very quickly."

The two sitting down think for a second and nod a yes to Eva. She heads for the ladder when Radek makes a suggestion.

"Oh! Can you make Oxen steak?" Radek asks with his mouth already salivating.

Eva nods her understanding and continues to climb down the ladder.

"With secret sauce?" Radek yells.

"No, we're not trying your sauce again," Eva says without a second thought. The last time Radek helped make a sauce for the steak it was combustible. He attempted to make it spicy which was highly successful. The after effects were not pleasant. When Evzen had it his mouth burst with burns all around his tongue. It burned even more coming out the other way, making him sit on the toilet all day.

As soon as Eva reaches the bottom floor, there is a knock at the front door. Without thinking, she snags the door open to see an unharmed Evzen, who has a huge smile on his face, and a battered Elliott holding a glass and metal container with a rusticly cut shock root.

"We got it!" Evzen screams triumphantly.

Just then, Marketa and Radek rush down the stairs, eyes lighting up with excitement.

"It was absolutely fantastic! We got chased by a studded raven, we dug through the canyon, and then we ran through the shock forest while a surge was going on!" Evzen summarizes.

Radek and Marketa seem to be intrigued by the looks of their jaws dropping. Eva, on the other hand, doesn't seem amused as she doesn't like the idea of putting them in danger. She especially looks over at Elliott, who is rubbing the back of his head with a nervous smile. The next thing she notices is the dry blood coming from the top of Elliott's forehead and staining the right side of his face.

Evzen, now being surrounded by his peers, continues to go into the details of their adventure. He uses various sound effects to describe the cry of the raven, the boom of the electrical surge, even imitating the roar of Chernak. He does this while also using hand gestures to visualize the events along with body movement like jumping up and down, as if he were some sort of ape.

Eva motions Elliott to follow her towards the back of the mansion in the kitchen. Above the plants, Eva reaches for a cupboard that contains medicine, bandages, and more medical supplies. She grabs a cloth, an anti-bacterial liquid bottle, and a bandage. She has Elliott sit down on a stool sitting next to the stove and begins to perform first aid.

She pours the liquid onto the small cloth to begin cleaning Elliott's wound. While wiping the scabbed cut on his head, Elliott winces as the anti-bacterial liquid does its job. Next she grabs bandages to wrap around his head.

"You didn't have to go, you know?" Eva says, breaking the silence.

"I know, but it was the least I could do. It's nothing, really," Elliott says.

"No, it's not nothing. Thank you for doing that," she says.

Elliott is left without anything to say. He winces again as the stinging comes back after Eva wipes over his injury again. Suddenly he begins to feel the aching pain in his arms and chest from the bludgeoning he took from the rocks. He tries stretching his shoulder but strains as moving it in the slightest edge causes a piercing pain.

Eva stops as she notices Elliott groaning in pain. "What in Heied's mane did you do?" she says.

"Let's just say it was a rocky start," Elliott says, chuckling at his own pun but is quickly cut off by his groaning.

"Take off the padding and the shirt," she says.

His eyebrows rose, surprised by the suggestion. "Are–Are you sure?"

"Oh grow up! Just take it off so I can give you treatment," she says. Although she won't show it, her heart starts to beat a little faster.

Elliott begins to unzip his jacket, revealing his dark green, waffle patterned long sleeve. Slipping his arms out of the armor is painful, feeling like the tendons and muscles will burst at any moment. Taking off the shirt is possibly the worst part. Elliott tries to pull the bottom half over his head, but the injuries in his shoulders and chest prevent him from going above his stomach.

Eva steps in to help, sliding the sleeves out with ease. Elliott's body is covered in bruises, making a green and purple colorization in the areas where he was pelted. Eva pauses at the amount of bruises scattered across his body, while also blushing ever so slightly.

She mentally tries to shrug off the feeling and reaches for the kit again for a cooling agent in the form of a gel. The agent is then applied to every point of Elliott's injuries with Eva spreading it in every wounded area. The next step is bandaging his chest and arms which she wraps thoroughly.

The entire time, Elliott cannot look away from her. He never noticed her light brown eyes, which seems to have a hint of green. She's amazing, he thinks. She's nothing like anyone he's ever seen. There is not a single person in the world he's ever met that is as pretty as her, he thinks. Suddenly he can't feel his injuries anymore, whether that be from the gel or from being captivated by Eva's beauty.

"Thank you again," Eva says. "For getting a root and protecting Evzen."

This is a new feeling, Elliott thinks. The appreciation is almost overwhelming, preventing him from coming up with any words to respond. The only thing that he is able to do is give a slight nod of acknowledgment.

Eva helps him put his shirt and armor back on, keeping it unzipped to relieve some pressure. The two of them head towards the third floor. At the ladder, Chernak waits patiently for his friend to join the rest of the group. Seeing Elliott come up the stairs with the crew's leader, a large grin comes from the dragon.

Well, what took you two so long? Chernak mocks.

Elliott points at his bandaged head. "I was treated for injuries, don't get too excited," he says groggily.

Chernak doesn't respond, but he keeps his mischievous grin while staring at Elliott as he climbs up the ladder. The silent stare seems to be more irritating to Elliott than the comment a couple seconds ago.

On the top floor, Marketa has already started installing the shock root into another glass cartridge and plugging it into the motor. She connects two wires on opposite ends, places it into a slot, then closes the engine cowl.

"All good to go!" she says.

Radek, who is standing next to the fuselage, puts on his blue cargo jacket. He slips on some fingerless gloves with a look that makes Elliott feel a little uncomfortable. As if Radek will do something questionable in a few seconds, making Elliott's skin crawl.

"Hey Elliott!" Radek yells. "Are you ready for the ride of your life?"

Elliott puts his hand in a dismissive gesture, "That's alright, I've got Chernak. He's always my ride."

"Oh come on. You should join us. We're stopping at the Infinite Geyser, so at least join us until then," Eva says.

"Yeah you should come with us! It'll be fun!" Marketa says ecstatically. Noticing the damaged mask hanging on Elliott's chest, she adds, "And I can fix that for you on the way."

Elliott detaches his mask from his armor, forgetting that it was still in need of repairs. "Oh no that's fine. I can repair it myself when–"

"Don't bother, think of this as a thank you. Plus I love repairing," Marketa interrupts, holding her hand out for the mask.

Elliott sighs and surrenders the mask to her. "Thank you," he says quietly.

Marketa takes the mask, observing the damage, and looks up again at Elliott. "Also I bet I can fix this faster than you," she says and walks away, preventing Elliott from retaliating. Instead he scoffs, followed by a slight chuckle.

"What's wrong with you?" Eva asks Elliott.

"Nothing. It's just . . . no one's offered me that before. Usually I would do my own repairs," he says.

"It's her way of saying she likes you. Don't worry, she'll take care of that mask like it's her own child."

Elliott laughs, "Good to know."

Radek unlocks the fuselage door, climbs inside towards the cockpit, and begins running diagnostics. Evzen stuffs rolls of maps and paper into his pack, along with botany materials like trowels. Marketa neatly places wrenches and screwdrivers into a handheld toolbox. Once she is satisfied they are ready and packed, she throws on an orange cap while closing the box to jump into the plane called Fiala. Eva brings bags full of food, medical supplies, and small cookware.

Elliott heads toward the hatch leading down the ladder, peeking his head down it where Chernak waits patiently.

What's the plan? Are you ready to go? He seems to say as he raises his head.

"Actually, I'm going to ride with them for a bit."

Chernak scoffs, *You're joking, right?*

"Normally I would be, but they insist on it. Plus, it'll just be to the Infinite Geyser. I'll just ride with them this one time and we'll be back to flying normal. It's a long journey anyway," Elliott reassures.

Although, Chernak doesn't seem too enthused as he growls and turns his head.

"Don't sulk about it, you big baby. Look, I'll make it up to you. I hear the crystal sharks are absolutely amazing," he offers.

Crystal sharks are native to the aquatic terrain of the Infinite Geyser. The reefs are where they thrive and continue to thicken their skin. They swipe their bodies across the coral the more they age. People fish for them, using their skin for candy and other kinds of sugar.

Chernak eyes his friend. *Why do you always know how to see right through me?*

"Because you're easy to read," Elliott teases.

His dragon seems to frown.

"Sorry, you're also easy to tease," he says as he stands up to walk back towards the plane.

"Attention Mere crew!" Radek screams, "The dome will be opening soon! Prepare for ascension!"

Everyone begins to scramble to pack the smaller pieces of equipment into the plane. Elliott helps Eva grab a couple tents and hammocks, loading them into the fuselage. Inside the plane, the passenger seats are evenly split, single-person and made of metal. There are three on each side, making the spacing fairly tight. Towards the back is a small door containing the backpacks and equipment.

Eva sits in the front with Evzen adjacent to her, Marketa sits behind Evzen and Elliott takes the seat behind Eva. There is a seatbelt for each person which they strap themselves in with. Radek takes the pilot's seat in the cockpit, of course.

"Alright!" Radek says, "For our new passenger, welcome to your first flight with Fiala! I'll be your pilot, the infamous Radek!"

"I don't think you know what that means," Marketa says.

Radek seems to ignore her. "In the event of an emergency, no need to fear. I will be saving all of your skins with my amazing skills. There are also parachutes under the seats if you feel like you don't have any faith in me."

"I feel like I'm not going to trust you before we even take off," Elliott mentions.

Although, it seems like there's nothing stopping Radek's announcement. "Without any further interruptions, let's get to the ride of your life!"

Starting the plane requires Radek to open his throttle, followed by turning the master switch and fuel pump on. Since Marketa has installed the shock root, the fuel pump starts the electrical flow. He presses a button on the top part of the controls which opens the dome. The top opens like large double doors, revealing the clear blue sky. The clamp holding the plane rises into the air where everyone can view the rest of the breathtaking city.

From there, he turns on the ignition to start the propeller. Fiala purrs and the propeller spins clockwise in hyper speed. Radek presses another button that causes a ramp to appear on the column just below the clamp and landing gear. It spans out like a large diving board for about four hundred feet.

"Here we go!" Radek screams. "Taking off in ten, nine, one!" Radek releases the clamp and the plane begins to pick up speed down the ramp. Elliott grips the seat and braces the ceiling of the plane. The buildings appear to move faster through the window.

Then suddenly, the feeling of the ground vanishes as the plane rushes off the ramp and begins to dip downward. Elliott tightens his grip, his stomach rises, and he holds his breath as the plane comes closer to the ground. This was a mistake, is all that goes through his head.

Radek quickly pulls on the throttle to lift the plane up while screaming, "WOOOOO!" The flaps of the wings extend, causing the aircraft to lift back up in quick succession.

The force causes Elliott to spring forward, nearly smashing against the back of Eva's seat. He holds the back of her seat and the edge of his, feeling like everything in his body is jostling around. Eva props her feet up against the wall of the cockpit to steady herself. All of the passengers scream in chorus just as they pass over groups of houses.

Radek guides the plane upwards while turning the control wheel with as much force as he can. The ailerons rise and the wings lower, causing the entire plane to tilt to the right, spinning drastically. Everyone lifts up out of their seat while the seat belt prevents them from flying out.

Elliott's stomach begins to churn. The only thing he can muster is, "Serpent's crystals," trying to hold in any bile rising in his body.

"Radek! You idiot! Knock it off!" Marketa yells in complete rage.

"What's that? I can't hear you over my wooing!" Radek responds. He steadies the plane for a second before he quickly spins the plane the other direction. They dip downwards again into the massive geo canyon heading east.

Chernak from behind watches in complete pleasure like he is watching a movie. He huffs and puffs like he is laughing. *You chose wrong, buddy.*

Radek pushes and turns the control wheel to make the plane travel down, up, left, down, up again, then right, and repeat. The vehicle proceeds in waves like a skateboard arch. Each passenger is lifted up and down the seat where whiplash begins to set in. Elliott, not feeling well at all, turns pale and close to vomiting his breakfast.

"Radek! You better knock it off now! That's an order!" Eva demands.

"Yes ma'am," Radek scoffs, bringing the plan in a steady, neutral position.

No one seems in worse shape than Elliott. His color starts to return but he holds his stomach, using every ounce of his energy to keep everything inside his system.

"How's your first flight, Elliott?" Radek mocks.

The new passenger gives a nasty look towards the cockpit.

As much as he wants to say the numerous insults popping in his mind, his body feels as if one word out of his mouth will result in puking. Although, now that they are at a stable angle, the churning in Elliott's stomach begins to settle down. But now the pain in his shoulders and chest returns.

"You're crazy," Elliott mutters. Then, as if Radek's laugh is contagious, Elliott begins to chuckle.

"You got that right!" Radek screams from the cockpit.

The laugh spreads as Eva and Marketa start laughing alongside Elliott. Mainly hysterical after managing to survive through Radek's impulsive piloting skills.

Miles ahead of them, further down the canyon, is an enormous cloud of vapor indicating that they will reach their first destination soon enough. Marketa sits the destroyed mask onto her lap, admiring the dents, severed wires, and leftover debris stuck within the mask.

"What did you do to this? Go mining?" Marketa asks Elliott sarcastically.

Elliott gives a wry smile. "You could say that."

"Well, it's going to take a while to solder the wires, fill and fuse the holes, pry out the dents, and the entire metal plains."

"You really don't have to do it, I can fix it and save you the trouble," Elliott says.

"Don't worry about it, I insist. Believe me, I can get it done before we leave the geyser," she says, as she opens a cartridge on her belt and fluidly flips out pliers like a butterfly knife.

The instinctual movement causes Elliott to make a physical reaction out of surprise. The gesture leads him to believe that she could probably fix the mask faster, not to mention better, than he can. She uses the pliers to pick out bits of rock lodged within the mask.

"So why are we going to the Infinite Geyser?" Elliott changes the subject.

"Oh! We're going to the Voda Svelto Festival! Once every year, groups of lightning fish come to one specific area in the city where they create light patterns around their homes. It's to indicate their end of the mating season and the females check on their young and eggs!" Evzen explains.

"It's also a place where there's casinos, games, and dancing. We could use a good time. Plus it'll give us time to stretch our legs," Eva adds.

Great so we're delaying the hunt again, Elliott thinks. Although, the festival doesn't seem familiar to him. Now thinking about it, he hasn't had any thought about visiting other traditions in other cities. So much time has been devoted to treasure hunting that he never thought about enjoying a game or a dance. Not very many at the least.

"Did you bring anything nice to wear?" Eva asks, turning in her seat towards him.

Elliott purses his lips, hoping that it's a rhetorical question, and shakes his head no.

"That's fine, we'll get you something. You'll get the best outfits where the festival is hosted."

"Honestly, you don't have to–" he tries again but is cut off by their leader.

"We'll all pitch in something. Right crew?" Eva says.

"Yes ma'am!" they say in chorus.

"I already have an idea!" Radek says.

"No you're not making him wear a fish bowl," Eva says as if reading his mind.

The pilot slouches in his seat in disappointment but his mood quickly shifts to excitement as he announces, "Alright people! We are about to enter the waterfall! You're gonna love this, Elliott!"

Everyone peers out of the window, observing the ever increasingly damp canyon walls as they glisten with crimson colors. Radek guides the plane closer to the wall and under the waterfall while a rainbow appears below them. Inside is like entering a new world. The entire wall is covered with beautiful, healthy, green vegetation growing with blue, red, pink, and yellow buds all on the left side of the plane.

On the right is the falls that seems to make its own aquarium. The transparent water reveals fish swimming with large fins on their stomachs and spins at the tips of each fin. Before Elliott can look at them closer, the fish swim towards the wall and hop out of the water onto the vegetation. Seconds after, thousands join in the same motion hopping from water to cliff and cliff to water.

"Look at all the cliff hoppers!" Evzen says ecstatically. "They're fish that jump to the habitats on the canyon walls to pick out pods and bugs. Then they jump right back into the water to enjoy their meal!"

Hearing the intellectual facts about the cliff hoppers, Elliott doesn't seem to retain any of the information as he is distracted by the elegant jumping of the fish.

Chernak, who is following just to the right side of the plane, becomes curious about the fish. Attempting to catch a cliff hopper in his mouth, he follows them a little too close to the water, getting caught in the downward force. Frightened by the water, Chernak flaps his wings heavily to catch back up to everyone else.

Seeing a division in the waterfall, Radek takes the plane out of the aquatic tunnel and ascends to find the city of Mestozmore. The wooden city is built on numerous, massive stilts in the middle of the water occupied by huts, docks, canopies, and rafts. Towards the further end of the city is the largest building with a pointed straw roof.

In the middle of the sea above the canyon is the famous Infinite Geyser spewing water hundreds of feet in the air. The radius of the geyser is so large it nearly blocks all the view of the horizon and the rest of the land. The sea that the geyser sustains sparkles with life, the ground below the surface of the water is crystal clear. Thousands of different types of coral and seagrass decorate the ocean floor with color.

Peering out of the window, Elliott can make out larger fish on the more still surface jumping out of the water in schools. Radek circles around the city, looking for the best place to land. While scanning the area, he finds an empty dock furthest away from the pointed straw building.

"Attention to all sirs and ma'ams, we will be landing in a few seconds. Please scream as loud as you can while we descend because this will be a fun ride!" Radek announces.

Elliott grips his seat and ceiling again. "Are we landing or are we crashing?" he says.

"We're landing either way! In this case we might be 'seaing', because it's water," Radek jokes.

"That's comforting," Evzen comments sarcastically.

"Radek! You better keep my plane intact!" Marketa screams.

"Her name is Fiala, thank you very much!" Radek screams back.

"Just land the damn plane, Radek!" Eva orders.

"Yes ma'am!" Radek responds and lowers the plane towards the dock.

They fall at a steep angle, causing Elliott's stomach to rise again. For a split second, everyone faces the water almost perpendicularly. Then Radek pulls up on the control wheel, extending the wing flaps, and skids across the waves. The force of the water causes the plane to bounce off the floats of the landing gear. They draw nearer to the docks at an alarming rate, seeming like they crash at any moment. Splashes of water sprout in the air, spraying onto the windows. Just until they think metal is about to hit wood, the plane comes to subtle slowdown.

"We have arrived! How much fun was that?" Radek asks.

"Can I request a new pilot?" Elliott asks Eva, semi jokingly.

"Believe me, I wish I could provide another," Eva responds in about the same manner.

Radek guides the plane on the water until they come to a stop. He turns the master switch off and the throttle in the rest position. Grabbing a neatly rolled up piece of rope while getting out of the cockpit, Radek opens the fuselage door and jumps out onto the dock to begin tying down the plane.

"No need to grab all the gear, just what you need for the night. Got it?" Eva instructs. "Let's have some fun."

Everyone unbuckles and exits the fuselage while bringing their own day packs. The docking area is just off the flat, wooden street where dozens of people walk along. Piers for fishing seem to be the main source of activity around here, complemented by several rafts and canoes. Small fishing huts sit on each side of the street with hanging, cylindrical shells along the corners.

Chernak sits near the street with a large grin on his face as he watches his friend hop onto the dock. *How was your flight with your new friends?*

Elliott gives him a snarling look. "Don't let me do that again," he says in a lower tone.

That bad, huh? Chernak huffs and puffs.

"I thought I was going to hork out my guts. I take back everything I said, we're flying together on the next stop."

Don't forget your promise.

"And I'll get you those crystal sharks, don't worry," Elliott reassures.

Suddenly out of nowhere, Evzen jumps from behind Elliott. "Hello again, magnificent beast!" he says while reaching to scratch Chernak behind the horns, who graciously accepts.

There's one thing I like about them. Chernak seems to say.

His friend shakes his head, chuckling at the sight of Chernak submitting to the horn scratches.

"Let's go play some games!" Radek says, practically hopping towards the road.

"Stick with the group, Radek," Eva says.

While walking down the street, the crew can feel the rush of the small waves beneath them that wash around the large pillars and stilts holding every structure together. The geyser is in perfect alignment with the massive straw building they walk towards, showing a great mist in the background like a mountain.

"Ah Mestozmore!" Evzen begins to preach. "The city of fish, goods, and entertainment. Many of the locals here believe that the shells beneath the surface represent each and every person. Which is why each hut has one or more hanging outside to express who they are!"

"What are you a tour guide now?" Marketa smirks.

"I can if I want," Evzen defends.

"Well then you should take us to a place to get something for Elliott to wear." She turns to Elliott, "Don't worry, I got something in mind that'll look nice and symmetrical."

Elliott says nothing and just looks at his reptilian friend who gives him a grin.

"Oh! And we can get something for Chernak too!" Evzen mentions.

Chernak's grin quickly turns into a frown. The moods seem to switch now that Elliott is smiling in amusement.

Everyone in the town seems to walk towards the main pointed canopy, conjugating around stands and stages. Several types of stands contain clothing sprinkled with shells, food roasted on sticks, and jewelry fitted with glowing strings. Their clothing consists of knitted robes and skirts.

Nearing one of the many entrances, the inside of the massive canopy is much more clear. Pillars circle the roof to provide structure along with one large pillar in the center. Rounding the middle wooden pillar is a glass floor showing the thousands of wildlife beneath the surface of the water. Fish glisten in the light, eels slither from pieces of coral to patches of seagrass, sharks with crystalised skin scan the ocean floor for food.

The smell of fried fish engulfs the air, mixing with the humidity of the geyser. Fish roast on grills seasoned with chilis grown on the sides of the cliffs. Cephalopods are slowly cooked on sticks over a fire for a smoky flavor. The most iconic of the festival foods are the crystal shark fins and rolls. Here the fins are cooled and stuck on a stick like a popsicle.

Games are set up throughout the area. Events that require tossing a bag into a bucket, blindly reaching in a pool for toy fish, and gambling for I's. One in particular is a game starting with a pile of coins in the middle in between two contestants. Those people use community coins to knock out as many coins in the pile from a distance as possible. While also having pockets on each end that they will try making a coin in to obtain tubes of gold coins that a player only has a limited amount. A game called Kapsa, which Eva eyes the gambling games with great interest.

Music begins to play off of wind and percussion instruments to create an upbeat, fluid melody. Performers on the stages come together first in a jumpy fashion then slowly turns into synchronized twists and kicks. They wear beautiful reflective dresses resembling some of the plants that wave in the water.

Flabbergasted by the sight of it all, Elliott's jaw drops while he admires the unfamiliar culture. While observing the events taking place, he almost doesn't recognize a little girl walking up to him with a necklace full of shells in the shape of a squiggled 'j'. She wears a teal dress lined with shells in the shape of a spiral almost making a flower. The lines of shells make a wave around her dress. Taking one look up at Elliott, the girl smiles while holding up the necklace and says, "At vas more vyzuvije," pronouncing every letter.

Elliott kneels down and accepts the necklace as she wraps it around his neck. She nods her head and skips away to her mother who waves at Elliott with a gracious smile. Overwhelmed with gratitude, he almost forgets to wave back.

The girl and her mother walk hand in hand towards the music and dancing stages.

"It means 'may the sea nourish you'," Eva says. "She's sweet. She wants you to be part of the family."

"I . . . I don't know what to say," Elliott stutters.

"Be thankful. Something like that comes a long way," she says, laying a hand on his shoulder. "Come on, we still have to find you some festival clothes."

Eva urges him towards a clothing stand on the outside of the massive canopy. Shirts, pants, headwear, shoes, and socks are hanging on stands and shelves. Selling the variety of knitted clothes is a man wearing a tan shirt, a fabric hat that sags to the side, and pants finely threaded in blue rhombus patterns.

As the crew approaches the stand, the owner opens his arms gracefully saying, "Welcome. What can I lend you tonight?" in a soft tone.

Eva turns to the rest of the group. "Everyone pick one piece of–"

"I call the shoes!" Radek interrupts.

Sighing in annoyance, Eva gestures for him to pick a pair out. "For Elliott, and don't be mean about it."

"Oh look at those pants!" Evzen blurts, running over to one of the stands. The pants he catches an eye for are a navy blue complimented by emerald green dashed lines. The fabric is silky smooth as Evzen runs his fingers across them.

Marketa and Eva look at each other with smiles, almost like they are telepathically communicating. In a split second, they move to the stands and shelves with the other guys of the crew giggling.

Eva searches through the shirts hanging in rows. Shuffling

through the clothing of all kinds of sizes, she pulls out a long sleeve, black button down shirt with a logo of a lightning fish in the top right of the chest. The noticeable feature of the fish is the large dorsal fin that is significantly larger than its body and longer than the tail. The color of the logo is yellow in the shape of a lightning bolt.

Eva compares the shirt to Elliott with one eye open. "I think this will do nicely," she says, handing it to him.

"And I think this will go with it!" Marketa says, holding a blue crown made of coral and tied with golden strings around the points. She lays it on the top of Elliott's head and says, "A good fit for a king."

Evzen comes close behind her to hand the emerald pants to Elliott.

Just behind him, Radek pops up in surprise. "Put these on!" he says ecstatically.

Flinching from Radek shoving a pair of shoes in his face, Elliott reluctantly receives a vibrant yellow pair of footwear with green laces that stand up like seaweed. He looks over towards Eva with a tilted head.

"Is this really necessary?" he asks.

Eva chuckles. "You'll have fun, I promise. Why don't you try it on over there and we'll find something for Chernak."

Elliott looks over at his friend who gives him a begging look. All he can do is smile. "I think it's your turn with them, buddy," he says.

You're a real pal. He grunts.

"I know I am," Elliott says, ignoring the sarcasm while he walks towards the dressing rooms that Eva gestured towards.

Chernak turns towards the rest of the group grudgingly

towards other stands outside of the canopy. Elliott presses the button on his pack to release Coil, who seems amazed at the overcrowding of people in many areas. The dressing rooms they head towards are small prisms made of wooden logs stacked on top of each other with no roof. Each one sits side by side at the edge of the canopy.

As Elliott opens one room, the most noticeable item in the room is a tall mirror followed by a bench with hangers sitting above it.

Closing the door, he lets out a long sigh. "Is all of this really necessary?" he asks Coil.

Coil jolts up as he creates a quick zip noise sounding like he's not sure.

The hunter takes one hard look at the festive clothes with appreciation. "You know, they are a good bunch of people. Maybe this trip won't be so bad. What do you think, Coil?"

The little bot makes a high pitched zooming sound with enthusiasm.

Looking at the pair of clothes again, Elliott laughs at the peculiar combination and begins removing his armor to slip on the new garments. The pants fit nicely with the smooth silk feeling significantly more breathable on the legs. The button up shirt is much more loose than the padded armor he wears almost all the time. Suddenly moving his arms becomes easier.

Putting on the wacky shoes is a little tight but has enough wiggle room for his toes. The laces still stand up after tying a double knot. The final touch is the crown Marketa picked out which rests comfortably on Elliott's head. Coil zips around to wipe off any dust and tighten the shoes as well as the pants.

"Well, what do you think, buddy?" Elliott asks.

Coil makes two consecutive noises with the first being higher pitched than the second like he's saying he looks handsome.

Elliott laughs and begins to gather his belongings to head back outside with Coil close behind. As they exit the dressing rooms, Elliott looks around to see Chernak walking back with the rest of the group. Large necklaces consisting of shells, orange and yellow flowers, with wavy blue ribbons dangling from his horns.

As they approach each other, Elliott chuckles at Chernak. "Bro, what happened?" he says with a large grin.

Have you looked in the mirror? Chernak mocks.

"Looking sharp, brethren!" Radek compliments.

"What do you think?" Marketa asks Elliott.

He takes another look at his friend. While observing, he tries to remember the last time Chernak had fun, much less smiling this much. It's amazing what a few strings of flowers can do, Elliott thinks.

"He looks great," Elliott mutters.

"Alright, now that we got you both something to wear, we have to change, too," Eva announces.

"Race you there, Evzen!" Radek challenges.

"You're on!" Evzen accepts as they both sprint towards the dressing rooms.

"Boys," Marketa says, rolling her eyes.

"Tell me about it," Eva agrees, walking towards the same direction.

Chernak plays with his necklaces and ribbons by hopping

up and down as everyone else walks away. *I think I'm starting to like them.*

"I'm not going to disagree with you on that one," Elliott responds. "While they're doing that, let's check some stuff out."

Can we get those crystal shark fins? Chernak seems to say, sticking his tongue out.

Elliott laughs, "Yes we can, let's go hunt for it."

It isn't hard to search for a food stand, much less one selling crystal shark fins, as they are spread throughout the area. The nearest one is about fifty feet away with a line quickly flying by. Several kids with their father dance around him with the fins on sticks. One kid in particular seems to have locked himself around his father's leg, who doesn't seem to care about dragging his kid around.

Chernak and Elliott reach the stand, both of their mouths watering.

"We'll take three please," Elliott says, handing a small bag of I's. "Keep the change."

The young, skinny, pale skinned man in a dirty, brown apron thanks him graciously. Each fin is about eight inches in length, covered in roasted crystal skin that gives it black shading to the normal blue and green color. Roasting the fins gives a smoky flavor that compliments the sweetness, making it taste a little like fruit.

Elliott hands two of the fins to Chernak. The two of them take one bite of the top of their fins. The food in their mouths burst with flavor, sweet, juicy, crunchy, everything about it is enough to make them crave more. They look at each other with satisfaction which quickly turns into lust as they begin to scarf down their candy on a stick. It's easy for Chernak as he eats his two whole, spitting out the sticks.

Not even reaching halfway through his candy, Elliott notices his dragon friend eyeing his unfinished treat.

With his mouth full, he tries to say, "Back off!" as Chernak begins to engage on the last piece. Elliott tries holding him back with his left arm, but the dragon is too powerful as they are able to knock him down. Chernak manages to take the rest of the candy and licks Elliott's face, causing him to burst into laughter and knock off his coral crown.

"You oxen butt!" he screams.

Have to be quicker next time. Chernak huffs and puffs.

The world around Elliott seems to slow down, becoming a blur centering around only one image. Wearing a beautiful, one shoulder dress of a green color on the top that gradually turns to a shade of yellow and orange is Eva. Her hair is styled with choppy bangs with a small bronze crown lined with orange petals. She walks over in sparkling sandals that seem to twinkle like the water in the light.

The image becomes distorted, the blur turning back to the real world as Chernak slowly moves in front of his captivated friend.

Wow, that's the most I've seen you drool. He seems to say, his sharp teeth showing his amusement.

Elliott, now realizing how long he had his mouth open, quickly stands up. "Shut up," he murmurs.

As Eva approaches the two of them, she gives Elliott a smile. "What do you think?" she says, proceeding to spin around to cause the dress to show off the elegance of it all.

"You . . . um . . . uh . . . look amazing," Elliott stutters.

"Thanks," she says, trying to hold back a big smile but is not very successful.

They stand in silence for a couple seconds until Elliott breaks the silence. "I appreciate the outfit, by the way."

"Of course. We couldn't let you stay in those ragged pieces of clothes," she teases.

"I'll have you know, those ragged pieces of clothes and armor have done me good for as long as I can remember."

"They've seemed to do good up until you have to look presentable," she retorts.

No words come up in his mind to counter the statement. Instead, Elliott scoffs humorously, shaking his head and cannot resist a smile.

Suddenly, as if they come out of nowhere, the rest of the crew pop from behind Eva. Marketa wears a maroon dress that fades from the bottom up with fabric sewn in the shapes of flowers outlined with gold and her curly blond hair dangles to the sides. Evzen has chosen a plaid dress shirt with different shades of blue and black pants to go with it. Radek, however, wears more of a vomit green and yellow shirt that literally looks like someone had puked on it, having inkblots sewn into it.

"WOOOO! Let's get the party started!" Radek screams.

Marketa looks at him with disgust. "Seriously, what are you wearing?"

"Think of it this way. If he does end up vomiting, no one would notice," Evzen says, trying to be optimistic.

Elliott gives him a puzzled look, squinting his eyes. "I don't think that makes it better."

"Elliott! I challenge you to a game!" Radek says with much liveliness.

The challenged hunter laughs. "Alright, pick the game," he says, following Radek further into the canopy.

Towards the center of the canopy there is much more activity. Various types of games are played on countertops and tables. These consist of dice, cards, disc throwing, fishing, shell stacking, drinking, dancing, and bottle flipping. All of this activity stands over the completely transparent, thick glass floor that shows much of the aquatic life.

Radek leads Elliott to an inclined board facing towards them with six distinct holes that create a pyramid. Three on the bottom, two in the middle, and one at the top, each row of holes gradually becoming smaller. Two sets of five small yellow and green discs sit in front of it. The object of the game is to reach a hundred points, the bottom holes equalling five points, the middle is ten, the top is fifteen. Each player takes turns tossing a disc about ten meters away.

"I call yellow!" Radek says, reaching for the set of yellow discs.

The two of them step back roughly ten meters and Radek starts the game by tossing one back straight into one of the middle holes. Elliott follows up by shooting one almost perfectly landing into the top hole. The challenger looks at him with complete surprise, leaving his jaw dropped.

"Alright mister 'I can do anything'! Looks like you're going to make me work for it," Radek says.

The two of them go back and forth in points, mainly making them in the top and middle holes. Although, each time Elliott throws, Radek attempts to mess him up with a quick yelp just before he tosses. None of them truly work but Elliott manages to fall behind with a score of eighty five and his challenger comfortably sitting at ninety.

Radek takes his next turn, who needs an exact number to win otherwise he is set back ten points. He tosses the disc in a large arc to land just next to the right middle hole and slides into it, securing his victory. He cheers triumphantly, dancing around his defeated opponent with his tongue sticking out.

Elliott, initially having a sour look, cannot help but chuckle at Radek's funny faces. "Alright, good game," he says, surrendering to Radek's triumph.

"Let's go see what the others are doing," the champion suggests.

Peering around for any recognition of a familiar face, Elliott finds a significantly larger crowd around a table. The spectators block the view of what is happening in the inner circle. He and Radek shuffle through the group to reveal a game of Kapsa. The contestants consist of a tall, broad shouldered, and fancy dressed man with short, light brown hair. He grins at his opponent who happens to be Eva, who doesn't seem too happy with the results she is receiving.

Her opponent in the suit takes two gold coins in between his fingers and the large, red community coin in his opposite hand. He flips the red coin with his thumb and, before it hits the table, flings the first gold coin in the small pile of I's that knocks just a few out of the circle. The second gold coin is tossed straight into the pocket sitting just in front of Eva just as the community coin lands.

Everyone on the man's side cheers for his victory, which he

responds by raising his hands with pride. Eva slams her fist on the table with frustration.

"What happened?" Radek asks.

"He just made his gold into the pocket. Meaning he took the last rod from her storage, which leads to him winning," Elliott explains.

The victor turns back to face Eva. "Don't worry, darling. I'll make your money worthwhile," he says.

Elliott's face quickly scrunches into disgust and anger. His words move faster than he could think, from pure instinct. "I'll take it before you can spend it."

Everyone falls silent to turn towards the direction of his voice.

"Oh yeah? And what makes you so sure?" he says.

"The fact that I'll take three rods on the first play," Elliott says confidently.

Everyone around them reacts with a long 'oh' realizing the challenge.

His adversary scoffs. "You're an arrogant one."

"Oh no, not arrogant. I just know what I'm good at, Mr . . . ."

"Bartolomej," he says, taking a slight bow. "If you claim to be as good as you say, go ahead and make your first move."

"Gladly. We'll play double what the last game was," Elliott says, setting down two bags of his own I's.

The closest people in gold jackets begin restacking the towers of coins in the middle for the next game.

"I'm sorry, I never got your name," Bartolomej says.

"Elliott, be sure to remember that name," he responds.

Bartolomej laughs. "You a friend of hers?" he says, nodding his head towards Eva, who stands just behind Elliott's shoulder.

"Yes, she is as a matter of fact."

"Good. We'll be close friends by the end of this," Bartolomej says, winking at Eva.

Snarling at the cocky gambler, Eva leans in closer to Elliott just above his shoulder. "You don't have to do this," she tells him.

"Oh I think I do. I've seen this guy for less than a minute and I already loathe him. I think you'd love to see him go bankrupt."

Eva can't help but smile at the image of Bartolomej losing. "Make him dirt poor," she says.

Elliott faces his opponent who holds the red coin in one hand, flipping it through his fingers. "Heads or tails, arrogant one," he says.

"Always heads," Elliott responds, as Bartolomej flips the coin in the air.

It clings onto the table, revealing a head of a fish, indicating Elliott's win on the toss.

Just in front of his twelve golden rods are his two tossing coins. He takes the two of them as well as the community coin. He flips it, tosses the first gold one towards the silver pile, knocking several of them out of the ring. The second one, however, is flicked towards the falling red piece, clattering against each other. The community coin then bounces and lands inside Bartolomej's pocket. By rule, the player who makes that kind of shot receives not one but three of their opponent's rods.

The audience around them cheers with complete astonishment and praise. Bartolomej, stunned by the swift and precise action, looks up at the young hunter who smiles with complete conviction.

"Like I said. I know what I'm good at," Elliott says, flipping the red coin in between his fingers.

Now having been silenced, Bartolomej prepares his coins and makes his play. He knocks far more coins out of the ring than his challenger and even makes one in the pocket, taking one of his rods. The crowd cheers behind him in retaliation.

Reassuring himself with his own skills, Bartolomej raises his eyebrow with interest. "How about we raise the stakes?"

"You want to lose more, I see. This will be interesting. What's your wager," Elliott asks.

The crowd chuckles at the comment. "I think your attitude needs to be checked. If I win, you have to swim with the fish below us. No coverings. It's not like you need that ridiculous outfit anyway," Bartolomej mocks.

"Hey!" Radek yells. "That is a beautiful outfit! Those shoe laces are so wavy," he says, sniffling.

"Calm down, Radek. I got this handled," Elliott reassures.

"He-he's mean," Radek stutters.

"I know, let me deal with him," he says, turning towards Bartolomej. "I'll take on your bet. She gets to choose what you will do once you lose," he says, gesturing towards Eva, who already seems like she has an idea.

"I think all of that hair needs to go. Eyebrows included, that way you'll really blend in with the fish," she says, viciously.

The smirk on Bartolomej's face slowly turns into a frown. "Deal," he says, gesturing for Elliott to take his next turn.

The play resumes with both players being quite precise with their shots, never missing the pile and hardly missing each other's pockets. In three consecutive rounds, Bartolomej is able to catch up and even surpass the amount of money Elliott received since the first. The stacks of coins in the pile dwindles to just a few lone pieces. The amount of rods in Elliott's possession becomes scant compared to the other player.

The smirk on the nicely dressed gambler returns as the odds seem to turn in his favor. "Mind the eels down there. They can get pretty nibbly sometimes," he says.

But the comment doesn't seem to phase Elliott. He just sits there with admirability, contemplating his next move. Eva, who has been watching with much concern, looks at him expecting a sense of defeat. Though, there is none to be seen in his determined eyes. He smiles at her and turns back to the game.

He takes the community coin to flip and throws the first piece at the diminished pile. The second one he aims at the red coin again, clanking metal on metal. The red coin falls right in Bartolomej's pocket again. Along with that, the coin he just launched bounces back straight into his own pocket. A move like that is highly unlikely and indicates an immediate victory for the player.

Astonished, everyone releases an applause and cheer from the sudden action. Bartolomej is shocked, his victory was just in his grasp. His heart races, not quite realizing what had just happened. While processing, the crowd then hovers around him with one person in particular with a razor and wax pads in his hands.

To Elliott's left are Chernak, Coil, Evzen, and Marketa all cheering for him after his amazing play. The victor takes his winnings and gives half to Eva who lets out a sigh of relief.

"I have to be honest, you had me scared for a second," she says.

"I know I did," Elliott responds, chuckling.

Eva brushes her hair over her ears. "You didn't have to do that, you know?"

"I know, but I think I just needed a fun game to play. Plus, that guy was out of line. He needed to be humbled," he says, as they hear the childish scream of Bartolomej being shaved and waxed, tearing the roots of hair from his skin just above his eyes.

Radek dashes to the rest of the crew bragging about how epic Elliott was and rants about how mean Bartolomej was towards the outfit. While doing that, Eva takes Elliott's hand, leading him towards the outside of the canopy where a dimly lit dock sits in between two small huts. The sky is now dark, revealing the bioluminescence of algae in the distance, creating a subtle green color to the water. Lamps dangle from posts on either side of the dock.

Eva guides him towards the end of the dock, leaning against a post while staring into the distance. Elliott takes the post opposite hers.

"I think that was the first time I've seen you that angry," he teases.

Eva sighs. "That guy was terrible. He tried flirting with me before I could get into a game. Then he went on to saying he wanted to be the one winning for me like some kind of knight. That's when I challenged him to a game," she explains.

"And then the true hero arrived," Elliott laughed.

She giggles. "Yeah, but I didn't need anyone to step in for me. I'm not a damsel."

"No, I wasn't saying–"

"It's alright. I can get pretty competitive, that's all," she interrupts.

Elliott nods with sympathy. "I understand that all too well. Were you always like that or did someone kick over your drink?"

Eva glares at him. "Are you trying to get a rise out of me?"

"No! I meant . . . I was just–"

She can't help but laugh. "I'm just kidding," she says. "I guess it was a bit of both. Most people I encounter think of me as someone who isn't good enough. I always felt like I needed to prove others wrong. Even to prove to myself that I can do what everyone else can and more."

They sit in silence. Elliott has no words to make a comment that seems appropriate. Nothing that seemed remotely comforting or anything relatable. Sure people have doubted his skills but has always seemed to manage regardless of what people thought.

"So why did you decide to become a hunter? Especially to get where you are now," Eva asks, breaking the silence.

She catches him slightly off guard. No one has asked that question towards him. "If I put it in a short statement, I really just like the thrill of the adventure. I don't have anything much better to do," he says.

"And what's the long version?" she asks, shifting her body so that her back is leaning on the post to face Elliott.

He takes a deep sigh. "I wasn't born in Rosbocovac. I come from Cernapisky just outside the Black Desert. I didn't know my parents and I don't know what happened to them. All I remember is that they gave me my name. I guess you could say I was alone for a large part of my life."

He turns his head back towards the canopy where Chernak dances with the rest of the crew who run circles around him.

"Then I met Chernak. I found him when I ran away from my hometown. He seemed like he was having the same problem as me. He was alone and hurt. From what I have no idea. But I took him in and he's been my only family ever since, with Coil of course. I built him so that Chernak wouldn't be alone sometimes, and to help on our adventures. But I mainly hunt because I need to support them, take care of them," he says, realizing how easy it is to talk to her.

Eva is speechless. The only word she can muster is, "Wow." From the corner of Elliott's eye, Eva swears that she can make out a tear hardly becoming visible in the dim light.

Finally, a question pops into her head to break the silence again. "Why the name Chernak? I've never heard that name before."

He tilts his head to the side, trying to remember when he named him. "It was the name of my grandfather, I think. I don't really know why I remember that name specifically. But supposedly he helped build the cities and design the system of hunting. But that's only what I heard rumors from people around town while I searched for my parents."

She nods with much interest. Elliott clears his throat to prevent any more awkward silence and asks a similar question to shift the conversation. "How did you and the crew meet?"

Eva chuckles just at the thought of the memories. "It was more or less the same way you and Chernak met. Radek was caught trying to steal food from a local food stand," she continues to hold back her laugh. "I helped him escape by dumping stinking sap on the owner. His face was hysterical."

"Marketa came from a strict family. Her parents wanted her to follow a code, become some kind of business woman but she was never interested in that sort of thing. She wanted to build stuff, get her hands dirty, all the things her parents hated. So she ran away and we took her in. She practically builds and repairs everything we have at home."

"Evzen was bullied when we found him. He would look for sphericals just outside the city." Sphericals are bugs that live within geos that they create in the dirt with their five legs. Two on each side of its body and one at its tail that are about the size of a finger. Their outer shell is their underbelly so that they flex and curve towards their back.

Eva continues with a sad frown, "He was pushed around because he loved admiring the animals and plants he found. Just for a passion he had, he was called fowl names and pushed over," she said angrily.

"What about you?" Elliott asks, now intrigued by the stories.

She hesitates, as if the memory frightened her. "My parents didn't want me. I seemed like a burden to them for a while. I never knew why. Then they locked me out of my home, told me I wasn't good enough and to get lost."

"That's horrible," Elliott mutters.

"Tell me about it," Eva says, wiping away a tear from her eye. "Now, just like you, I take care of the crew. I take them to events like this so that they can have fun and bond like a family. There are two kinds of adventures. Those that are for the thrill and those that are for the love. Both are what this crew is all about."

Taking a moment to let the last part of the speech settle in,

Elliott can't help but think about his good pal and the hunts they have been on together. But realizing that he never had the opportunity to see him act the way he is right now, dancing playfully with the rest of the party to the cheerful music.

Suddenly, a quick flash of yellow appears in the water. Then another that is green, and another orange. Everyone under the canopy begins to gather around the middle peering through the glass floor.

"It's starting! Come on!" Eva says, pulling Elliott by his hand.

The lights are turned off to admire the natural light show below. The fish creating the streams of light are almost too quick to spot the shape. Lines of bioluminescence paint the water in various shapes as if someone was taking a brush to outline an image. Soon enough, the canopy is lighting up again but by the lightning fish that have come to check and protect their eggs.

The group on stage begins to play a slow melody. A man and woman in silk clothing play flutes harmoniously while a drummer keeps a soft beat. The lute and ukulele join in the chorus and main stream. The people who have gathered now pair up to dance slowly to the music.

Eva urges Elliott to dance with her, in which he takes her hand to pull her closer. He leads to the beat, swaying and stepping side to side to catch the rhythm. Once synchronized with the music, they seem to dance with the streaks of light and their unique shapes.

She pulls him closer until her head rests upon his shoulders and her arms wrapped around his neck. His hands slowly reach around her lower back, interlocking his fingers. Before he knows it, his head rests against hers while they dance in the night light.

6

THE BLACK DESERT SHOWDOWN

The smell of cooked seafood and the rush of waves on wood is what wakes up Elliott. After the festival, each member of the crew rented out a room at an inn nearby called the Sludge Fish Inn. Everyone seemed to have passed out as soon as they made it to their rooms.

His room is small but clean. Sanded wooden floor boards lay out the frame with a neatly cut dresser depicting the geyser and a bed from which he rises out of. The white, soft blankets only covered half of his body since the atmosphere was slightly humid. A mirror hangs directly across from him where he notices one side of his hair sticking up.

Suddenly he hears a knock at the door that startles him saying, "Breakfast is downstairs when you're ready. We'll head out right after."

It sounded like Eva's voice. The memory of last night comes to Elliott's mind. The lights, the music, the dance especially. His stomach starts to flutter. Am I hungry or is that a different feeling, he thinks.

Sluggishly he changes back into his original outfit and armor. After walking out of the room and down the stairs, he sees the rest of the crew sitting at a table with empty plates and steaming beverages in polished clay cups and plates. The dining room is scarce with only a few people not including the crew sitting at tables and the bar to the left of the stairs, who greet him a good morning.

Chernak waits outside with his head sticking in the window. *Nice of you to join us. And it was even nicer to not hear your snoring.* The dragon snorts.

Elliott gives a scornful smile, still trying to wake up. "I don't snore," he replies.

"What was that?" Marketa asks, not quite hearing what he said.

"Nothing," Elliott says, sitting down in between her and Evzen, who hands him a plate of food and drink.

"Oh don't worry, I talk to the air sometimes, too," Radek says, out of pocket.

Everyone stares at him, each thinking a similar thought about what makes him this way. Elliott shakes his head, ignoring the comment and focusing on his food and drink.

Marketa lightly taps his shoulder to grab his attention. "I have a surprise for you," she says, reaching under the table and handing him his mask. It looks as if it is brand new, not a single scratch visible.

As Elliott takes it, it seems different somehow. Before he can ask the question, Marketa continues. "I may have added a few modifications. Adding to the normal visor, you can now switch to a thermal recognition by flipping this switch," pointing to a tiny lever near the temple. "Also, given that we are sitting right over an ocean, I decided to install a respirator and air seal. I'm surprised you didn't think about that already."

Elliott now realizes the circular filter at the mouth. "I guess it never crossed my mind," he says, slightly irritated at the comment. "Thank you," he manages to mutter after looking into the ecstatic eyes of the curly red haired mechanic. "So what's the plan?"

Eva stands up, gesturing to Evzen to bring out a map of Poclad. She points towards the south east where a large body of water indicates the Infinite Geyser. "We're right here and our next stop is Cernapisky," she says, now moving her finger more towards the middle, east of the grassy plains that says Soundless Plains and just outside the Black Desert.

"We'll stop to stretch our legs for a second and then head towards Mount Spiral," pointing towards the top right corner in the north east where a spiral mountain range is indicated. "We will probably stop at Studeny Brazina just above the Swamp Mountains," indicated at the edge of the continent toward the east. "There we will have to go through the Burning Iceland and go straight into the mountains where our treasure should be waiting for us."

Elliott nods in understanding and looks to his buddy through the open window. "Looks like we're going home, pal," he says.

Chernak stands up, sticking his tongue out in excitement. *Are you going to choose wisely and ride with me this time?*

Elliott scoffs, "You already know."

Marketa leans towards Radek. "Is it just me or does he actually think that the dragon is talking?"

"I don't know, I think I'm starting to understand him," he says.

She sighs, "Why did I even ask?"

After finishing breakfast, Eva instructs the crew to clean the table and start packing the plane. Now having some food in his system, Elliott walks side by side to Marketa. "Where did you learn to repair and build like that?"

"Oh I learned on my own! It's just easy for me to figure it out. And once I do, I never forget how to do it again," she responds.

Reluctant to ask his next question, he asks, "Do you think you could teach me some pointers?"

She turns towards him, her face lights up with exhilaration, gasping, "Of course! I would love to! Gamorat's tusk! I've been wanting to show someone these things but no one is interested!" she says, mentioning a deity in the Hyperfreeze Forest that takes a journey to the Burning Iceland to spread joy.

"Well great! Once we get to Cernapisky I think it'll be a good place to practice."

"Perfect! Oh boy! I can't wait!" she says as they approach Fiala the plane.

Everyone loads their belongings into the plane quickly since nothing else was unpacked. Everyone except Elliott, who hoists himself on top the saddle of Chernak, attaches his improved mask onto his chest, and waits for the plane to start. Eva closes the fuselage door once ready.

"Next stop, Cernapisky! Hope you all brought coverings

cause we're about to get more than just a tan!" Radek announces in the plane.

"You mean a burn?" Marketa says.

"I prefer to say a char," Evzen mentions, as he slides a straw hat on his head.

"Here we go!" Radek says, pressing the master switch again, preparing the plane for takeoff.

As the propeller spins, spraying mist of water in the waves, Radek salutes to Elliott indicating that they are ready to go. Elliott salutes back and urges Chernak to launch off the wooden platform. Fiala pulls forward away from the dock, the floats skid across the water that make the plane fly up and down the waves. They arch up and down, splashing water in the air until finally she rises up off the surface.

Shifting the ailerons, the plane turns toward the left where the geyser sprouts water as tall as a mountain and as wide as five cities. The light in the water refracts to reveal a large triple rainbow.

"Who wants to take a little dip in the water?" Radek says from the cockpit.

"If the water wasn't scalding, I'd probably stick my head out," Evzen says.

"You're going to give me a heart attack one day because you're screwing around with my plane!" Marketa says annoyed.

"Trust me, you'd be able to fix it in a day or two, it doesn't matter what he'll do to it," Eva reassures.

Meanwhile, Chernak leads Elliott just behind them who is intending to do the same.

"Hey, why are we not going around the geyser?" Elliott asks, worrisome.

Relax, we're going for a little soak. Chernak yelps.

"That's not a soak, that's a burn!" he yells, folding his mask onto his face.

The plane takes the first dive into the steaming water, covering the windows with hot fog and pelting droplets. Elliott shields his head with his arm, thinking that the water would burn through the armor. The air around him becomes significantly warmer, but nothing that penetrates the skin as his entire body is covered, exactly what the armor is intending. The scales on Chernak's body prevent any damage to himself, making him impervious to heat.

Now dripping with water, Elliott removes the mask after they exit the geyser, "You idiot! I could've baked in there," he says laughing.

Without the mountainous geyser blocking the view beyond, the black, sandy dunes of the Black Desert are revealed just past the ocean. A dark beach connects to the water, picking up sediments along the way. To their left is the rest of the Geo Canyons and plains that have several rocks and boulders that the waves crash into.

As they approach the heated terrain, Elliott pulls out a brown desert scarf that he can put over his face, just below his eyes. The tail end of the scarf flaps in the wind behind him.

Within the plane, Evzen is the one to start the conversation. "So is Elliott going to be part of our crew now?"

"I like him! After seeing his game last night, I'd gamble with him any day," Radek says.

"I'm not sure. It all depends on what he wants," Eva says with a smirk.

"I'd want him with us. That way I don't have to be the only one building," Marketa says, crossing her arms.

Everyone is silent for a moment until Evzen breaks it again. "But you love building," he says.

"I know I do, I'll never stop," she says, almost cutting him off. "But it would be nice to teach someone some skills."

"Hey! I wanted to learn," Radek complains.

"You just wanted to play with the tools!"

Radek laughs maniacally after that comment.

The crew now hovers over the Black Desert, leaving behind the geyser miles away. The heat becomes dry, causing the metal of the plane to heat up significantly like an oven. The wind at least compensates for it while Elliott endures outside. He observes the seemingly never ending sea of dunes across the land.

Then something catches his eye. A shining object reflecting in the light followed by cascading debris around it. Nothing is very recognizable as they are so far in the air. But one is quite distinguishable. Someone is lying in the sand face down, most likely unconscious.

"Oh damn, Chernak, get us next to the plane," Elliott says, tightening the reins.

Flapping his wings harder to catch up side by side to the small aircraft. He waves his arm in the air to grasp their attention, which is successful. He uses his hands to gesture to keep moving, pointing in the direction of Cernapisky. Then uses his index fingers and have them meet together in order to indicate that he will meet them there.

He pulls the reins on Chernak to start descending towards

the collapsed person. As they drive closer, Elliott can make out more of the details. Now he can see that it is a man sprawled on the sand. His clothes are dark and wrapped in rags that are slightly singed. The equipment around him are cases of finished rations, empty water bottles, and used prospecting tools such as a shovel that seemed to be what caught his attention in the first place.

Chernak softly lands on the loose, black sand and Elliott jumps off to check on the man. It takes some effort to roll him over, but his face is burnt from the heat. Blisters form around his eyes and his skin is bright red, beginning to peel. That means he hasn't been unconscious for long, Elliott thinks.

Then another thought strikes him. This man is someone he knows, named Jiri. He was a neighbor back at home who was quite kind to him. He was the first person Elliott asked about his parents and grandparents. Even provided food and supplies for his journey before he met Chernak.

Back on the plane, Eva grabs a parachute from underneath her seat. "Keep flying towards Cernapisky. I'm going to see what's happening," she says, as she opens the fuselage door which causes some wind to catch on the inside.

Eva straps the parachute to her back and jumps out without hesitation, pulling the chute once she gets closer to the ground.

Marketa closes the door. "How can she just jump out like that? You'd have to strap me down, knock me out, and push me," she says.

"Are you afraid of heights?" Evzen asks, mockingly.

She gives him a dirty look. "No, I have a fear of falling. There's a difference."

"I don't think there is," he says.

Eva slowly reaches Elliott, where he pours water onto Jiri's face. Jiri blinks his eyes several times but does not manage to wake up completely. As soon as Eva lands, she presses a button on the bottom of the pack to bring the chute back in to be reused.

Elliott turns his head to see Eva surprisingly. "I tried to tell you guys to keep going, I don't know if I was clear enough. Probably not," he says.

"They'll meet us there. I got your message pretty clearly," Eva responds, kneeling down next to him. "How can I help?"

Wanting to refute, Elliott realizes there is nothing he can do as she is still here with him. "We need to get him to the city. He's had a heat stroke and several burns. Help me get him up."

Just as they begin to lift the man up, Chernak quickly turns attention to something. He sniffs the air and digs his claws in the sand. The ground rumbles while a stream of dirt kicks up. A massive creature, about the size of Chernak, travels through the sand and jumps out with its powerful jaws. Another sand dragon dives for Elliott and Eva.

Just before they become lunch, Chernak jumps in its way, ramming it in a head-on collision. The pursuer, not expecting the hit, is sent tumbling to the ground but quickly stands back up to face his opponent. The other dragon is slightly darker and bigger than Chernak.

"We need to move! This is going to be ugly!" Elliott yells, beginning to drag Jiri away from the fight.

As the two hunters heave the man off the ground, the two dragons lunge at each other. The wild one chomps down onto Chernak's neck, piercing through scales and flesh. He roars in pain trying to shake off his attacker, throwing it in the vicinity of the others.

The wild dragon crashes down on the sand, where Eva and Elliott throw themselves on the ground to take cover. It rolls over to take another shot at the people avoiding the battle. Before the beast could reach for them, it feels a sharp pain on its tail where Chernak has grabbed with his claws and teeth.

Chernak drags the beast on the ground and swings it over his shoulder with all his strength. The body of the dragon slams onto the ground with a puff of sand. It releases its tail from Chernak's grip and burrows itself in the ground. He does the same to chase after it, kicking up sediments and causing the terrain to shake.

Elliott and Eva quickly take Jiri by the shoulders, dragging him towards the direction of the city. The sand beneath them vibrates violently. Elliott turns them sharply left just in time for the fight to burst from beneath and miss them by a hair. They bash their heads together with Chernak doing his best to keep himself in between his assailant and his friends.

The wild dragon shoots its head up to crash against the underside of Chernak's chin with its horns. Chernak is caught off guard with his head shot upwards by the strike. Taking advantage of the fight, a massive set of jaws bites down on his left wing. The sharp pain leads to a shriek of agony, rupturing tendons and severing muscles.

Eva leads the unconscious man and Elliott further away, just out of the way where Chernak rolls over the beast to knock it loose. Now in a standoff, the two reptiles prepare for their next move, both growling, snarling, and hissing. The darker one spreads its wings to make it look bigger, standing on its hind legs.

Immune from being intimidated, Chernak bends his head down and turns it to the side. It seems the wild dragon has the upper hand, realizing the position that his opponent has taken. They don't seem to be ready to serve any attack. Noticing its advantage, the beast dives down towards the back of the neck for a killing blow.

Just before it makes contact with him, Chernak snaps his head up with his horns and crashes into the bottom horn of the dragon. A loud crack echoes through the air and the bottom horn of the bigger dragon falls onto the hot sand. It screeches in pain, turning away from the fight. It looks back at the victor, who releases a terrifying roar, as if telling it to back down. The now sad and defeated beast turns away, walking in shame.

Chernak turns towards his friends. *What a punk.* He snarls.

"Are you alright, buddy?" Elliott asks, concerned.

It's just a couple scratches. He whimpers, trying to keep his balance.

Elliott looks towards the horizon where a glimpse of the city can be seen, reverberating in the heat. The problem has now just escalated. With Chernak in his condition, they can either walk towards the city with the little supplies they have while also carrying Jiri. Or they can make a break for it on Chernak, who is hurting and has to struggle to carry three people. If they end up walking, there might not be enough energy to make it to the city, and they have no way of contacting the rest of the crew.

"Chernak, do you think you can make one quick trip to Cernapisky with all of us?" Elliott asks his friend. "I don't want to push you."

The dragon nods his head. *I'll be fine. You know me, I'll push myself anyway.*

"Push too hard and you'll hurt something more important. I'll grab some medical supplies and a treat once we get there."

Motivation! I like it! He snorts.

"Chernak," Eva says, resting a gentle hand on his face. "Thank you," she says, locking eyes with him.

Something about her makes the mighty reptile tear up. Her warmth brings pure joy to his heart. He turns to Elliott, *Alright, I'm not going to lie, I see why you drool.*

His friend purses his lips and cocks his head to the side. Then he gestures for Eva to help him lift Jiri onto the front part of the saddle. Once his stomach rests on it, Elliott jumps up and gives Eva a helping hand to have her sit just behind him.

Chernak grinds his teeth due to the weight of them irritating his wounds. He flaps his injured wing, pushing through the pain to lift off the ground. The searing sensation envelopes through his body, especially through his wing. The damaged wing causes them to dip down, slicing through dirt. He flaps harder to keep his elevation up but it only increases the pain.

They bob up and down with the passengers watching the neck and wing drip with blood. The closer they approach the city, which is significantly more clear now, the more Chernak strains to stay up.

"Keep up, pal! You're almost there! Keep going!" Elliott encourages.

"I see the plane! Just outside the city!" Eva yells.

The great sand dragon breathes heavily, pushing with everything that he has left. With the city in sight, there is no way he will stop now. For a moment, every feeling of agony goes numb for a few seconds. Chernak thinks about nothing but reaching the plane and making sure everyone on his back is safe.

Quickly they come across the city and his wing cannot take it any more. It gives out and the four of them tumble onto the ground just inside the city and past the plane. The area around them becomes covered in a cloud of black dust. Elliott slides across the ground with something heavy lying on top of his stomach, making it hard to breathe.

Waving the dust away and coughing, Elliott moves whatever is on him. As he touches it, he realizes it's Jiri who is mumbling something incomprehensible.

"Are you guys alright?"

"What happened?"

"Nice landing!"

The three distinct voices of the rest of the crew becomes audible, especially Radek's voice. As the dust clears, Radek is seen helping Eva on her feet while Evzen and Marketa come to help Elliott. The two of them roll Jiri off him.

"Get him to a fountain, he needs water," Elliott mutters. "Now!"

The two of them don't argue nor hesitate. They put Jiri's arms around their necks and swiftly carry him towards a fountain that gushes with clear water.

The city is small as well as its buildings made of clay and stone that is a much lighter tone than the sand, most likely from the Geo Canyon terrain. Tents are a common place for people to sleep under. Roofs and cloth canopies shade much of the area to protect people from too much heat. Several fountains of water have been placed in distinct locations with large umbrellas above them to provide more shade. The fountains serve as their irrigation systems as well, leading to shaded crops and turbines for power. The people living here walk around with rags around every portion of their body, only leaving the eyes uncovered.

Elliott first makes sure Eva is uninjured. When she confirms she is alright, he immediately turns to Chernak who is exhausted and in much agony. He evaluates his wounds, peering at the large gashes in his neck and wing. Scratches on his leg have almost gone unnoticed as well.

"Is he going to be alright?" Eva asks.

"He needs rest, a lot of it. But none of this would kill him. It was a typical dragon challenge and if he didn't knock off the other's horn I don't know what would've happened," Elliott explains.

"Why is knocking off a horn significant?" she asks.

"It's a sign of dominance in a fight for them. Once a horn is broken they submit and the winner becomes the alpha. I guess that dragon wanted more than just food."

"So there was a fight? And my boy won?" Radek interjects. "How wavy is that?" he says excitedly.

Elliott sighs. "It's not wavy that he's hurt," he turns to Eva. "I'll have to stay with him for a while. You guys can go on and maybe I'll catch up."

But Eva is already opening her pack, pulling out a medical kit. "No, we'll stay here to help him recover. Both of you are just as much a part of this crew as any of us right now."

Meanwhile, Marketa and Evzen grab buckets of water from the shaded fountain to sprinkle onto Jiri's face. In due time, Jiri slowly regains consciousness beginning to reach for the rest of the water.

"Don't be hasty, sip the water. Don't chug," Marketa demands.

The shaky hands of Jiri grabs hold of the bucket, almost forgetting what she said and takes large gulps at first.

"What were you doing out there by yourself?" Evzen asks.

"I feel like that's a dumb question. He was probably hunting."

"F-f-or . . . fa-fa," Jiri attempts to talk with an incredibly dry throat.

"What's he saying?" Evzen says.

"Oh let me translate in dehydration. How am I supposed to know? He didn't even finish his words," Marketa says, passive aggressively.

Evzen grunts. "Do you always have to be so mean?"

"Do you always have to ask stupid questions?" Marketa retorts.

After taking another swig of the ever so delicious water, Jiri mutters, "Fa-mily."

"Oh sphericals, he was providing for his family! Where is your home?" Marketa says, waving her arms in the air.

The man lifts his arm, pointing his finger past the fountain and down a large alley.

"Elliott! He's awake," Evzen announces.

The other three shoot their heads towards the sound of his voice. Radek immediately darts towards his comrades, while Eva gestures for Elliott to go check on him. She tends to Chernak's wounds with clean rags and antibiotics.

As Elliott walks over to Jiri, who seems to have completely awakened, he recognizes the young hunter with great content.

"Elliott? Is that you? You've grown!" he says, his throat becoming more clear by the second, his voice being higher pitched.

"Hey Jiri, how are you feeling?" he says, relieved.

"Much better now. I was meaning to take a swing at a hard treasure, what a trip that was. I didn't realize how far I traveled, so that led to me not realizing how little water I took, silly me," he says.

"Silly you, indeed," Elliott says, under his breath. "Can we take you home?"

"Oh please, I'd be happy to provide food for you as well."

"Food! I'd love some!" Radek says, spreading his arms in the air.

The group escorts Jiri past the fountain. He seems to be able to walk on his own quite fine. Not many people wander the streets of Cernapisky. The only ones being people harvesting crops, selling items, or getting water.

"So how do you know Elliott?" Radek suddenly asks.

"Oh we go way back. He was a boy when we first saw him, skinny little thing he was. We gave him food and some tools when he wanted to leave for his first treasure hunt. What was it you were after again?" he says, addressing the question to Elliott.

"A Rezeirdium Egg, a hard treasure. Bugs that cover their eggs in saliva to make it stronger," he explains, quickly trying to pick up the pace.

"And healthier, I'm familiar with Rezeirdia," Evzen says. "You did a whole hard treasure by yourself? How old were you?"

"I was about twelve. I wasn't totally alone, I had Chernak," Elliott mentions, now frowning at the thought of his state.

Noticing his sorrow, Marketa puts a hand on his arm. "Isn't

there a type of medicine or herb that we can get for him around here?"

"For who?" Jiri asks.

"For our friend, he's hurt badly."

"No, unfortunately nothing around here that can be much help. There are the typical antibiotics but nothing major," Jiri says. "Oh right here," he points towards a small, rectangular hut made of clay. Windows made of straw are forged with the sediments.

Elliott knocks on the wooden door and immediately a fairly beautiful woman opens the door. Her skin is dark and her eyebrows thick but small lips. Gasping at the sight of Jiri, she embraces him while she sobs softly.

"I thought you dead," she says, sniffling. Her accent is as beautiful as her, elegant and smooth.

"I'm here now, my love. Luckily I had help," Jiri says.

She looks at everyone there. "Thank you so much!"

"You're quite welcome!" Radek says without hesitation.

Marketa gives him an agitated look.

"This is Dorota, my lovely wife," Jiri introduces. "My love, could you grab some food for these kind people."

"Oh that won't be nec–" Elliott begins.

"Don't be silly, my dear. It's the least we can do," Dorota interrupts.

"WOOHOO FOOD!" Radek says, barging into the household.

All of them walk into the small hut with little furniture. The entire building only contains three rooms. One space for a nearly empty living room, another for the kitchen that has a small oven and stove with a large metal pot. The last must be a bathroom.

The living room is empty except for a crib in the corner with a sleeping baby wrapped in a blanket.

"Who is this?" Marketa asks in a soft but high pitched tone.

"That's little Marek. Please be gentle, I just put him to sleep," Dorota says.

Elliott helps Jiri to a stool where he rests against the wall. He cannot help but think about Chernak. "Dorota, do you by chance have anything that can help patch injuries quickly?"

"I'm sorry but we don't. You are welcome to ask the people but there is not much," she says.

His heart sinks, knowing that there isn't anything but whatever Eva has in her pack. It might be enough to stop the bleeding, but not enough to relieve pain or help heal any faster.

"Oh!" Evzen pops in, remembering something. "We are next to Lake Fatal. There is an herb there called Leceni Kelp used for rapid recovery."

Just like that, Elliott's spirits are lifted. "Great! How do I get it?"

"That depends. If you're lucky, there might be some growing along the shoreline."

His heart starts to sink again. "And if I'm not?"

"You'll have to get it from within the lake, full of corrosive acid. The name really speaks for itself."

7

LAKE FATAL'S MAGICAL HERB

Lake Fatal is a deadly place. The lake is so unbelievably corrosive that people believe the acid continues to eat through the rock and stone beneath. One drop of it would tear flesh and bone away in seconds. Some creatures are corrosive resistant like Chernak that thrive around the area, feeding off the vegetation and even living within the lake. The journey to get over there by foot is not much of a problem. The lake and the soil around it is the bigger situation.

Elliott quickly walks back towards Chernak and Eva, where it seems the bleeding has stopped. The blood that has fallen into the sand is hardly noticeable and most of it seems to already have evaporated.

"How is he?" Elliott asks as Eva caresses Chernak's neck.

"He's resting now, the poor thing. He'll need it for a few days," she says.

"Maybe not for that long," Elliott mentions, making Eva turn her head towards him. "Evzen says there's an herb in Lake Fatal. He said it was a lany . . . or lenny . . . something that would help him heal faster."

"Oh well we can start grabbing things from the plane and–"

"No, I'll head over there on my own. He's my responsibility," Elliott interrupts with a stern voice, tightening his pack straps.

Eva straightens up to meet his eye level, placing her hands gently on his cheeks. Looking past his anger and sternness, she can see concern, desperation, and sadness in the tears that begin to well up in his eyes. His lips quiver and he does his best to hold back his sadness.

"I feel like I failed him," he says. "I should've been the one protecting him."

"No you didn't fail him. There wasn't anything you could do. What I saw back there is that he loves you very much. I know he would trust you to make the right decision," she consols, brushing her thumbs across his face.

Elliott closes his eyes to let her words sink in, now wishing that her hands never leave his face. He takes a deep breath and nods an understanding.

Once her hands leave his head, Evzen and Marketa enter their presence.

"Where's Radek?" Eva asks.

Marketa scoffs. "He's waiting for food to be made at Jiri's. Don't worry, I told him to behave and help out."

"As long as the food gets done faster, he will help out," Evzen adds.

Elliott tightens his scarf and begins to walk towards the north side of the city. Before he could take more than ten paces, Marketa stops him. "Are you going to Lake Fatal? If so, can I come?"

He hesitates, not quite knowing what to say next. As much as he wants to go on this expedition on his own, the words of Eva echo in his head. The concern in Marketa's face looks quite familiar. She seems as worried about his friend as he does. He takes one more look at Chernak lying in the dirt and then back at Marketa.

"Alright, fine. Come on," he says.

"Yes!" Marketa screams, darting for the plane to retrieve her pack full of tools.

"Watch over him for me. I promised him treats," Elliott tells Eva and Evzen.

"I promise," Eva says.

"I won't be long, buddy," he tells Chernak, who is still sound asleep.

Marketa comes back with her toolbox that she holds by the handle. To Elliott's surprise, she takes the handle, presses a button to release straps that turn the box into a satchel. Satisfied that they are ready, they begin their walk just past the small, clay buildings and into the plane of black and red rock.

Most of the terrain is flat sitting on the transition from the Black Desert on the east to the Geo Canyons on the west. The ground is much more rough, crackling as the two hunters walk. In the distance, wind moves the sand and dirt into small funnels. Dry bushes cascade around the area that only reach about ankle height. Ahead it grows darker in the clouds, making the setting much more gloomy. A perfect environment for a place called Lake Fatal.

"Are you alright?" Marketa asks.

Not noticing his fists clenched, Elliott loosens his grip. "I'm fine. I just want to see Chernak soaring again."

"I wish I could have a pet," she says.

"Oh Chernak isn't a pet," Elliott refutes. "He's been my family for a long time."

"Oh I'm sorry, I didn't mean to offend."

He chuckles. "That's ok. People might think I'm just talking to an animal. But he's more than that and I can't quite get away from him."

A gust of wind brushes over the valley, nearly placing sand in their eyes.

"So how are we going to harvest this herb?" Marketa asks.

"I'll have Coil identify it and hopefully just be able to pick it from the shore. If not I'll have to dive into the lake," he explains.

She squints at the thought of jumping into an acid filled lake. "Can your armor take that?"

Elliott waves the thought away. "Don't worry, I actually infused this armor with the scales that Chernak sheds. The strength isn't as strong as it once was, but the resistance to corrosive materials is still there . . . In a way, he still protects me even if I'm miles away from him."

"That's smart! If you want, I could show you how to create more reinforced armor. It'll be like plate mail," Marketa says enthusiastically.

"That would be great!" he says. "Just out of curiosity, how did you get into mechanics and smithing?"

The pony-tailed redhead thinks for a couple seconds, never having to answer a question like that for a long time. Remembering the memory, she laughs at the thought. "It was a long time ago. As a kid I was fascinated by the idea of putting two or more things together and making something new out of them. Eventually, I wanted to make a submarine drone. Don't tell the others this, but I named him Suppy," she says, giggling over the name.

"I didn't get to use him very much. My deadbeat father crushed it with his feet. And my mother supported him!" her cheeks begin to turn bright red.

"Serpent's crystals, I'm sorry," Elliott empathizes.

Marketa shoos the thought away. "Don't be, I'm happier with the crew. At least I'm not restricted with what I can do."

Elliott realizes, the more he listens to the stories they tell in this crew the more attached he seems to become. A feeling of acceptance is something new to his heart. The overwhelming feeling causes him to smile.

"Don't ever tell the others I told you any of that!" she says, pointing a finger in his face, scaring him out of his trance.

"Hey I'll forget it once we get back," he says in a surrendering manner, making her restract.

Elliott looks forward, not realizing how long they have been walking. Once the image registers in his mind, he puts his arm out to slow Marketa down to a halt. A herd of oxenrock linger around eating geos from the dirt. They are burly creatures with two large horns sticking out of their head horizontally. Their fur is thick and full of dust that has been picked up from wind pushing into it. When their bodies shake, a cloud of sediment poofs up in the air. Some are smaller than others, more than likely are the babies land children. The hooves they use for shoveling out their food are wide in a rhombus shape.

"I don't need Evzen to tell me that oxenrock are highly territorial," Elliott says. "Just follow my lead."

He slowly starts walking around the herd at a safe distance with Marketa falling in behind. They carefully place their feet in the softer portions of the ground, avoiding the dry brush. The oxenrock ahead that don't have horns give glances towards them but pay no mind to the wanderers. Most of them grab a perfectly spherical geo and crunch onto the rock and bugs inside with their mighty jaws.

Marketa admires the babies walking around the mother, the horns indicate the female. The two children she has play together, swinging and bashing their heads together with the occasional hop to gain the upper hand.

Marketa cannot help but say, "Aww they are so cute!"

Elliott looks behind at her, taking extra caution at what she is peering at. "They're cute alright. Just don't look at them for too long," he says.

But before Marketa can take action, the mother glances at her with great fury in her eyes. She snorts a puff of air out of her nostrils and begins walking towards them.

"Don't move!" Elliott directs in a commanding but quiet tone. "And keep your head down, now!"

Marketa listens, breathing rapidly out of fear. As the beast comes closer, she shakes her head indicating that she is ready for a fight.

Ever so slowly while the oxenrock is paying attention to Marketa, Elliott takes off his pack to reach for a small bottle full of clear liquid. "Stay calm," he says. "I've got it."

Closing in around forty meters, the mother stops. She snorts again but this time stomps her hooves, scraping them against the dirt to prepare for a charge.

Working quicker now, Elliott digs in the ground for a geo

which can be found with a darker tone in one spot of the ground. Marketa still has not moved a muscle. Every second becomes more terrifying than the last. A geo is found by Elliott, who pushes the sand away from the rock beneath.

Then, the oxenrock begins to charge, leading with her long, sharp horns. She lets out a low grumble and stampers on. Elliott pulls out the sphere of rock, dowses it with the clear liquid with a squirt, and dashes in front of Marketa who is closing her eyes and tensing up.

He holds out of the geo as far as he can while looking down and away from the mother. Just before she impales her horns into her target, the oxenrock stops in place. Her eyes gaze upon the geo, sniffing it intensely as she makes a low groan. Elliott tosses the geo away without looking, leading the mother away and feasting on her delectable food.

Without hesitating, Elliott snatches Marketa's hand, leading her away from the herd towards the lake which is just up ahead. The scared mechanic finally opens her eyes, looking around to see where they are.

"Wh-why did she charge?" Marketa asks.

"I think you made eye contact with her. It's a call for a challenge, especially when she's near her children," Elliott explains.

"What made her stop?"

"I used some spherisum, a pheromone that is released by the sphericals so the oxenrock are more attracted to them," he says.

"I feel like I'm talking to Evzen," Marketa claims.

Elliott laughs. "I guess you guys have grown on me," he says, without thinking.

Marketa blushes, feeling proud from the comment. Realizing

what he had said, Elliott clears his throat as if something forced him to say it. Gulping, then clearing his throat again, he tries to break the awkward silence. "The lake is just up ahead."

The environment becomes more of a marsh. A heavy fog rolls over the area, giving a ghostly setting. Buzzes, clicks, hisses, and groans fill their ears with noise. The humidity is so thick it is almost hard to breathe. Every step they take causes their feet to go deeper into muck and mud. When they raise their feet, oozing materials drip off their shoes. There is almost no color as everything here is dark and deep green. Much more vegetation grows around the mud, sprouting in limp and depressing vines and leaves.

Straight ahead of them is the calm Lake Fatal. The shoreline can reveal some forms of kelp and grass, but beyond that is just murky acid. No water in sight.

Elliott pulls out a spray can from his pack, sprays himself with it, and hands it to Marketa. "We don't want to be bitten by any rage flies. You won't be happy afterwards," he says, intending the pun.

Marketa takes the can to spray herself. "How often have you come here?"

"Plenty of times, actually. This spot is big for some extreme treasures inside the lake. Around the marsh you won't go anything lower than a hard one. Too many bugs, the lake will kill if you're not covered, not to mention corroded wolves," he explains.

"Corroded wolves?"

"Yeah, biggest canines you'll find and probably one of the most terrifying predators on the continent. Not quite sure if they'd be scared by anything."

"Comforting. Now you really do sound like Evzen," she mocks.

Elliott then presses the button to release Coil, who hovers towards Marketa to say hello. "Hey, pal. I need you to see if you can find any lebony kelp."

"Leceni kelp," Marketa corrects.

He shakes his head, "Whatever."

Coil then hovers swiftly towards the shoreline, just about ten meters ahead. His white light indicates the scanner for anything he can recognize. He then flies back towards his companions, shaking his head with a saddened low zip sound.

Elliott's shoulders tense. He closes his eyes, scrunches his face, and lets out a long groan. "Serpent's . . . CRYSTALS!" he screams, scaring most of the wildlife around them.

Coil, flinching from the sudden uproar, shudders up and down like he is crying.

"Oh damn. Coil I'm not mad at you. I'm just annoyed at the circumstances," Elliott reassures.

"What's the problem?" Marketa asks.

"The kelp isn't on the shoreline. So, what Evzen said is that I have to dive into the lake to look for it," Elliott says, gruffly.

"But haven't you done this before?"

"Yes, but it doesn't mean I like doing it."

"Then why are you a treasure hunter?" she asks, rhetorically.

Elliott grunts, then digs into his pack for a large stake with a cord and hook attached. The pointed end of the stake seems to be able to detach in four segments. He chooses a spot in the ground and stabs the stake with as much angry force as he can. Then he presses it into the mud with his boot until it reaches the top where the cord is. He then pulls it to release the segments at the bottom, attaching the hook to the back of his belt.

"Is that all you're using?" Marketa asks.

"That's all I really need. All I really have," he says.

"Let me help with that," she says, opening her toolbox. She pulls out a thick rod with a screw point at the end. It is a similar anchor system but seems more secure. "You're a famous hunter and you use devices like a caveman."

Elliott shrugs, "Alright, we'll see which one works best," he says, holding out his hand for the hook.

But Marketa is hesitant, but eventually forces herself to hand it to him. She takes the anchor and presses a button for it to begin drilling into the mud.

"What was that?" Elliott asks, narrowing his eyebrows.

"What was what?"

"You hardly letting me touch the thing."

"I um . . . just don't want you . . . ruining it," she mutters.

He gives a look over to Coil, who gives him a high zip followed by a low one like he is unsure.

"I promise I'll try to be careful," he says. "I will give two tugs on the cable for you to pull me up. If the cable is pulling too fast it means I'm being dragged."

"Dragged by what?" she says, becoming worried.

"Well there could be a number of fish. One thing I'm really worried about is a boil squid," he says, a giant cephalopod that uses its tentacles to heat the water or acid in this case to practically weaken and cook its prey. "But what you should worry about is any corroded wolves around the area. If there does happen to be one nearby, lie in the mud out of sight."

"I'll keep it in mind," she says.

Once hooked into both anchors, Elliott checks his armor and sleeves to ensure no part of his skin is showing. He slips on gloves that are air sealed to his sleeve. Coil provides another container much like what they used for the shock root and hangs it onto his friend's belt. Now satisfied, he places his improved mask onto his head, covering the last exposed part of his body.

He then beckons Coil to follow him towards the lake. The mud becomes far more thick now it is mixing with the acid that fills the lake. None of the corrosive liquid is able to break through the resistant armor. He trudges through until the acid reaches his waist. Elliott releases a long sigh, inhales deeply, and dives into the lake.

The lights on his crossed shaped visor turn on and Elliott closes and opens his fingers to make them webbed to help swim. Coil swims side by side to him, scanning for any sign of the leceni kelp. It is murky throughout the acid, but the few things they can spot are schools of double dorsal finned fish, eels burrowing into the muck, nothing much that appears dangerous.

The further towards the center of the lake he swims, the deeper it becomes until a gaping hole becomes apparent. The pit of darkness below sends a chill down Elliott's spine. Fish roaming around the hole are much larger than the minnows along the shore. Their heads resemble that of felines, with long, sharp needles for teeth. Others have thin bodies that zip through the acid and stop themselves immediately with their fins that act like wings or parachutes.

Coil guides his master deeper into the pit, where he excitedly beckons him. Deeper and deeper they travel, the darker it becomes. Luckily, the white light from Coil's scanner is easy to follow in this crevasse. Several plants cascade around this area. Some that are thick and sprouting with spikes around its center. Some that are tall, rising up near the surface with wavy petals along the columns.

The small droid comes to a stop ahead of Elliott, showing a beautiful green patch of kelp. The plant is protected by a glistening clear sack around it. It seems to dance with the current around them, waving in a graceful fashion. Elliott swims over just in front of the kelp, beginning to pick at them to place in the container hanging by his hip.

***

Back on the surface, Marketa watches as the cable continues to extend until it comes to a stop. No sign of a tug or rapid pull so no need to pull him up, even though he can swim upwards but it is only to help him.

Staring at the anchor begins to irritate her eyes, forgetting that she needs to blink. She looks up and around the area to keep her eyes away for a couple seconds until something stops her. Marketa's body freezes at the sight of three, massively built canines in the distance walking towards the lake. Their skin is nearly bare, their veins glow a pale green that pulsates through the fog.

She remembers what Elliott had said if she saw one, crouching low to the ground to hide herself in most of the grass and weeds. The most terrifying part about the corroded wolves are their eyes that glow the same tone as their veins. But their pupils are pitch black and can be seen from meters away.

===

Ten pods of the leceni kelp seems to be enough. Elliott closes the container when he feels the acid around him move. Not by any common fish that he has seen coming down here, something bigger. Peering around the murky pit does not help much as there seems to be nothing.

Just before he clasps the container back onto his belt, something slithers up his leg. Then suddenly grips and pulls hard on him, dragging him further into the depths and dropping the container in the process.

Before him is a boil squid, large tentacles, cylindrical head, and a beak strong enough to pierce through metal. Elliott tries to shake, kick, thrash out of the tentacle but nothing works. It only appears to make it angry enough to start heating the acid around them.

The container falls towards the squid. Coil swims without hesitation to retrieve the kelp as quickly as possible before it becomes lost.

===

The cable quickly loses most of the slack. Marketa presses the button at the top to reel it in but the machine has a hard time. Grinding the gears as much as the anchor can, it doesn't seem to be enough to pull Elliott back to the surface. Suddenly the mud the anchor is holding starts to rise, losing its grip.

Just as it comes loose, Marketa dives for the end, causing it to pull her towards the lake. With her quick thinking, she taps her belt buckle to activate an emergency cable at the back of the belt. It shoots out with a crack, planting itself deep into the mud and just catching something strong enough to hold her right above the shore. The hair dangling from the sides of her head singed from the acid.

Her hands hold onto the anchor as hard as she can as she takes a rope from her pocket and ties herself to it. The corroded wolves gaze in her direction.

Now both his legs and an arm are entangled in the boil squid's grasp. The heat emitting from the cephalopod starts to make its way through his armor. While it is able to withstand the acid, the heat raises his body temperature. But now the possibility of breaking the armor is imminent.

Coil is able to use his robotic arms to grab the kelp. He pulls the container back towards the surface, dodging the several limbs of the monster.

Continuing to battle the aquatic beast, Elliott draws a pointed device that vibrates vigorously and injects it into the tentacle holding his right leg. He holds it in to ensure it lets go. Once he gets the rest of his limbs free, the anchor system pulls him upward. The cable drags him through the dirt below, covering him in all sorts of materials. His vision becomes blocked by everything he runs into.

Marketa regains her balance, but is now lying in the mud hoping the wolves do not spot her. Sniffing and snarling, the canines approach the vicinity of her. Just about twenty meters out, her heart races thinking that she's going to become dog food.

Just before they spot her, the cable brings in a figure covered in kelp and muck. It raises its arms as it rushes out of the acid, roaring with rage and pain. The corroded wolves that were just looking for their next meal lose their appetite, whimpering at the fear of an unknown creature.

They all quickly turn their heads to the opposite direction, sprinting away from this new predator. One of them may have let some urine loose along the way. Elliott brushes off the sediments and debris from his body while Coil comes over to him with the container full of leceni kelp.

"I got it!" Elliott screams. "I got it," he says, panting.

Marketa gasps for breath after holding onto the anchor for as long as she did. Her fingers and arms ache from the strength of the boil squid beneath the surface.

"I think it's safe to say that we were both wrong about the anchors," Elliott jokes.

8

THE SMOKE CLOUD HIVE

The sky becomes burnt orange in the evening. The area around Cernapisky becomes much tougher to see in the black sand, seeming like it will blend in with the night. Eva starts to drift into a slumber while leaning onto Chernak's back. Her head dips downwards only to snap back up as she tries to fight the urge.

Just then, Chernak wakes up groaning and snarling in pain. The sudden motion is enough to bring Eva to her feet and dash towards his face.

"You're awake!" she says. "Elliott will be back soon, he's grabbing medicine for you right now with Marketa."

Chernak lifts his head, hearing what she had said. He looks around to see if he can find his friend anywhere.

"He'll be back soon, I promise," Eva consols.

The dragon nods his head and rests it back down to the ground.

"Alright, now I am starting to believe him. Can you actually understand me? I just have to ask."

Again, the dragon nods and snorts a puff of air into her face. She laughs with disbelief and petting his face afterward. Evzen and Radek walk in their vicinity after checking on Jiri and Dorota.

"How is he?" Evzen asks.

"He's awake, still hurting though," Eva says, sighing nervously. "I just hope they make it back soon."

Radek and Evzen glance at each other smirking, thinking the exact same thing. "Eva?" Evzen says, "Do you like Elliott?"

Her eyebrows shoot up and her cheeks turn bright red from the sudden question. "What? What do you mean? What makes you think that? Maybe? I don't know! Why are you asking so many questions?" she says frantically.

"You asked the questions," Evzen mentions.

"Uh oh!" Radek butts in with an even larger grin than usual. "Looks like our great leader has a crush on–Thwaah!" He couldn't get any further as Eva slaps him across the face, leaving a big red hand print on the side of his cheek.

Chernak huffs and puffs hysterically, contagious enough to make Evzen laugh as well. Their laughs quickly come to a halt when Eva gives a dirty stare towards both of them.

"Please don't slap me, but speaking of which," Evzen says, pointing up ahead towards the fountain where Marketa is helping to pour water over Elliott's acid-covered armor.

The gunk attached to the armor dried quickly walking back from the lake. Although, it seems to wash off just as quickly every time Marketa splashes Elliott with water.

"I think you're fine now," she says.

Elliott unfolds the helmet, bringing it back to its original spot placed on his chest. He thanks her and rushes over towards the group standing around his beloved dragon friend.

He hands the glass container holding the kelp to Evzen. "Can you make the medicine for him?"

"Without a doubt," he says, now digging through his pack to pull out an herbalism kit. He specifically grabs a mortar and a pestle to crush up the herbs.

Elliott, eager to see his friend, walks towards Chernak. "How are you doing, pal?" he asks.

I've been bitten and I can't stand. I think I'm good. He grunts.

"He'll feel tons better after he tries this," Evzen says, holding what once was the herb and is now a paste. He places half of the paste inside Chernak's mouth, who swallows quickly. He then scoops the rest of the green paste in his hand and rubs it onto the wounds on his neck and wing. The dragon growls in pain, causing everyone around him to flinch. Everyone except Elliott, who knows him too well. "Now we wait until morning," Evzen says.

"How early? Do we need to do anything else?" Elliott stammers.

"I'm not sure. But I am sure he will make a full recovery."

Elliott sighs heavily not realizing his shoulders were so tense, feeling like a great weight has been dragging him down. Suddenly a large slap on his back causes him to stumble slightly.

"Nothing to worry about here anymore! Now we should worry about food!" Radek says.

Elliott chuckles, "I like where your head is at . . . currently. But hit me like that again and I'll make sure the red print on your face turns purple," he says.

The pilot throws his hands up in a surrendering fashion. "You got it, dragon rider. Now let's get some food!" he says, dashing back towards Jiri's hut.

"Are you coming?" Eva asks Elliott.

"I'll stay with him, I've been gone long enough," he says.

As he sits beside his friend, Eva can't help but show a look of empathy. "You're very sweet, Elliott. I'll bring you something."

The rest of the group enters the small house where Dorota pours a very dark brown stew into thin wooden bowls. Jiri holds his son, Marek, in his arms to prevent him from crying. In fact, the little baby laughs as his father makes playful noises. The place feels musty but the smell is worth it, filling the air with marinated broth, cooked vegetables from the garden, and meat heating from beneath the ground in the back side of the house.

Dorota hands the bowls to each of the members of the Mere Crew. "Here you are, my dears," she says.

They thank the owners and Eva grabs a second bowl for Elliott, beginning to head back towards him and Chernak. The rest of the crew sit around the small table, drinking the soup from the bowl.

"So are you a hunter?" Marketa asks Jiri, who managed to put the baby to sleep in his arms.

But he shakes his head. "Not much of one, no. Not like Elliott who seems to be known all throughout the capitol."

"Then why were you out in the desert?" Evzen adds.

"Oh well, we don't have much, you see? The gardens are one of our main sources of food and work, but not much pay. We don't hate it here, not one bit. But I wanted to get a big load of money for my family, for our son in particular. We want him to have a good life, you know?"

"He will have a good life. He just needs you in it, my love. Which is why I did not want you going out there," Dorota says.

"I promise, I will not do it again," her husband says.

She leans in for a kiss and takes their baby from Jiri's arms to put in his crib.

———

The sky is completely dark now with only a few lanterns dimly lighting the fountain. Eva brings the steaming bowls to Elliott and sits just beside him.

"You two seemed like you had fun," Eva jokes.

Elliott laughs. "More or less. I don't think I could've done it without Marketa. She's a great teammate."

"She is. She seems to admire you. They all do."

"Sometimes I wish I could be better though," he says. Another thought comes to mind after his comment. A question that he wishes he can say out loud but cannot find the courage to do so.

Instead, Eva takes his hand, holding it close to her. "They don't look up to very many people. They need someone like that."

Sighing softly, Elliott nods in understanding. The two of them sit in silence as they sip on their soup. Eventually drifting off into a deep sleep hand-in-hand.

———

The two hunters, sound asleep, eventually begin to fall backward. What they were once resting against moves, forcing them to wake up to see Chernak flapping his wings. The once injured dragon is now jumping up and down, shaking the sand beneath them. He gallops around the fountain without any sign of strain or pain. He roars just as he pounces in the air, gliding around the city.

Elliott and Eva cheer with relief, embracing each other from an act of instinct. Elliott's legs feel like jelly, as if the weight of every coin mined from the Metallic Plains has left his shoulders. As soon as Chernak lands where he once slept, his friend wraps his arms around the dragon's head. The wounds have completely healed, not a trace of a scar anywhere around his body.

"That sounds like the magnificent sand dragon I remember!" Evzen says, running out of the house with Radek and Marketa close behind him. The rest of them gather around Chernak, thrilled to see their favorite companion flying once again.

Jiri and Dorota walk out to see the crew petting, patting, even kissing the mighty beast. The two of them admire the dragon in awe, not expecting a predator that lives in their land to accompany a group of humans.

"I must be still hallucinating in the desert, honey. I think I need water," Jiri says to his wife.

She chuckles, "I must be imagining the same thing."

"What is that kelp? Can I get some of that?" Radek says, causing everyone to laugh.

"No you can't," Eva says. "I think it's safe to say we should pack up, everyone!"

All the crew members cheer in chorus and begin to grab their belongings to prepare loading onto Fiala. Jiri, who is still damaged from the burns of the desert, approaches Elliott.

"My boy, thank you for saving my life," he says, pulling Elliott in for a hug.

"It was nothing," he says, clearing his throat.

"It was everything," Jiri says, facing him again but holding him by the shoulders. "I would not be able to help my family if I had died. If anything, they may have suffered as I have. No treasure is worth as much as what I have right now. Protect what you have, Elliott."

The words spoken by Jiri ring through his head like a bell. So much so that he cannot come up with any words himself to respond. The only thing he can do right now is nod in understanding. The gardener taps him on his shoulder and bids him good luck.

His wife embraces each member of the crew, eventually coming to Elliott last who thanks her for the food. In due time, Radek powers the plane after everyone has loaded into it. The propellers spin vigorously, creating a cloud of black sand. Elliott hoists himself onto Chernak's saddle, signaling to Radek that they are ready to go.

"You ready, buddy?" Elliott asks.

Hell yeah! Never felt better! He roars.

Fiala is guided around the city of Cernapisky and Radek pushes into a higher velocity. Soon enough, the plane takes off with Chernak soaring just beside them.

"Next stop Studeny Brazina!" Radek announces the name of the city in the northern parts of the Swamp Mountains.

The small, dusty town begins to appear smaller as they fly further away towards the northeast portion of the continent of Poclad. Lake Fatal starts to disappear as well, the dark marshes evaporating as the dirt feeds into the Black Desert towards the east. North of the lake dissipates into an enormous cloud of fog covering the entire region. A place called the Smoke Cloud.

It becomes impossible to see the ground, the smoke reaches heights higher than the plane can reach. No one exactly knows what lies in this region. The gas that creates this cloud is highly poisonous to humans. Most likely feeding from the fumes of Lake Fatal's minerals and acidic liquid.

Radek faces the plane towards the Smoke Cloud without any thought to turn around it. Eva notices his lack of maneuvers, she leans over her seat. "Hey, Radek. Are you planning on taking us through that cloud of death?"

"You know it!" the pilot says.

"I think it would be less idiotic to fly around the cloud," Eva says in a passive-aggressive tone.

"Radek!" Marketa screams. "You better not break my plane! The more damage you do to it, the more damage I'll do to you!"

"To 'her', thank you very much!"

"And here we go again," Evzen says, rolling his eyes.

"What was that?" Marketa says, snapping her head back towards him.

Evzen's eyes burst wide open, not expecting anyone to hear him under his breath. "Nothing! I was just saying that we should . . . uh . . . wash the plane after we land," he says followed by a nervous laugh.

"I like that idea," Radek comments.

Eva grunts, "The point is, we should really go around the cloud. It's an unnecessary risk to go through it."

"Trust me, Eva, it'll be fine. Going through the cloud is a

much faster route than around it. So I would recommend everyone putting on their gas masks," he says.

Still not enjoying the idea, Eva and the rest place their masks on their faces in case of any gas sneaking inside the plane. Each mask is sitting under their seats. A filter covers where the mouth should be whereas the rest of it is a visor. A seal outlines the mask to prevent exposure with a strap around the temple and cranium.

From outside the plane, Elliott begins to realize everyone in the plane is putting on their gas masks. "So we're going through the Smoke Cloud," Elliott says.

That'll be fun. Radek must love not seeing. Chernak snorts.

"He's crazy, and I'm not opposed to it," he chuckles, placing his own mask over his face, lighting the crossed shaped visor.

The cloud appears much larger as they fly closer, appearing as a wall of fog about to engulf the plane and the dragon. Soon enough, the both of them disappear into the mist. Elliott guides Chernak to stay close to Fiala so as not to lose her. The cloud blocks most of the light outside from beaming inside. There doesn't seem to be a trace of anything in sight. The ground is completely out of eyesight, no sign of natural features, nothing that appears to be moving. All there is is dark mist.

While flying for a few minutes in the toxic cloud, a snap comes from within the plane which causes it to vibrate. Clanking can be heard coming from the engine.

Radek flinches from the sudden snap. "Well," he chuckles anxiously, "I can't really ask for a new set of pants since I only brought one pair. Ladies and gentlemen, I think we have a problem."

"WHAT DID YOU DO?" Marketa screeches.

"Don't worry! I'm sure whatever it is we can fix it quickly," Evzen says.

"Who's this 'we' that will fix it?" the mechanic asks, angrily.

"You're right, you can fix it and it will be ten times better."

"Land the plane now, Radek!" Eva demands.

"I would if I could see!" the pilot says.

From outside, Elliott observes the front part of the plane for any sign of damage. Whatever the sound was, it wasn't due to external forces. Although, there is a repetitive clunking noise coming from the engine.

"We need to help them land, buddy!" Elliott says to Chernak. He urges his dragon towards the front of the plane, staying cautious of the propeller. Elliott grabs Radek's attention, waving his hands in a motion to follow him. As soon as the signal is understood, Elliott guides the plane down at a slight incline.

"You're going to see the ground before I do, so let me know when you see it," Elliott says.

Chernak nods, keeping a close watch on the ground. Nothing seems to show itself. That is until one large feature appears just ahead of Chernak, who reacts just in time to dodge out of the way. The sudden change in direction nearly causes Radek to crash, but turns the wheel just in time. The ailerons shift and the wings turn the plane at almost a perfect ninety degree angle to continue following the dragon through the mist.

Not much of the feature is visible, only that it seemed large and immoble like a mountain. Trying to see through the mist, Chernak can make out a hint of land that seems roughly flat. He screeches to let his rider know of the ground. Elliott creates a stopping motion with his hand to let the pilot know he needs to prepare to land.

Radek pulls up quickly to level the plane. Fiala then strikes the ground, the landing gear bumping up and down on the rough terrain. For the most part, the ground is dry as pebbles jump up from the force of the vehicle. The plane comes to a stop in what looks to be a clearing. The mist is thicker than ever, since this gas appears to be dense enough to stay on the ground. Not a tree, animal, nor large rock structure in sight. Although nothing can really be seen over thirty meters.

Elliott jumps off Chernak as soon as they land, rushing over to the plane. The first thing he hears is Marketa grunting, snarling, and cursing under her breath that he can't quite decipher. All he knows is that they must not have been nice words.

"I'm keeping my promise to you, Radek. The wrench and the hammer are screaming your name! The wrench will be for your teeth and the hammer for your legs!" she screams through her mask as she begins to open the fuselage towards the engine.

"What happened?" Elliott asks Evzen.

"We don't know, something with the engine. Marketa said something about cylinders, fuel pumps, I don't know. Not my field of expertise," he explains.

"Whatever it was, it didn't sound good from outside."

"I'm sure it's fine," Eva says. "Marketa is just very sensitive about her things."

"I'm not sensitive! I'm protective! There's a difference, especially when you have a brick-head for a pilot," she insults.

Radek jumps out of the plane as she finishes her sentence. "I didn't do anything, Fiala is the one who is a little sick."

Elliott and Evzen look at each other questioningly. "I shouldn't be too surprised. I was the one who saw him hold the wedding for himself and the plane," Evzen says.

Elliott laughs, "Please tell me you were the best man."

Evzen looks at him amusingly, knowing he doesn't have to answer that question verbally.

Marketa opens the fuselage door to the engine where she first looks at the reciprocating engine, the portion where the shock root is connected. The engine itself looks intact, so she draws her eyes all around towards the pistons. It is this portion where the problem arises. The connecting rod to the pistons has severed into two pieces.

Marketa releases a large sigh. "I found the problem. You got lucky this time, Radek. It was just the connection rod."

"What happened to it?" Eva asks.

"It snapped in half. And I was hoping this wouldn't happen after I installed the shock root. It must've put too much stress onto the pistons which, you guessed it, destroyed the connection rod."

"But you can fix it, right?" Evzen asks, trying to stay optimistic.

"I can't fix it, but I can replace it. Just give me a while to break it down and install another one," she says.

"Do you want help with that?" Elliott asks. "We can call this my first lesson," he says, trying to cheer her up.

"Sure, thank you," Marketa asks, softening her tone.

The mechanic retrieves her toolbox and a spare connecting rod from the back of the plane where she keeps most spare parts that they might need. With her trusty wrench, she begins unscrewing the parts of the connecting rod. The piece itself is a metal stick with a ring on each end, one smaller than the other connecting to the piston. The larger ring is clamped down with two screws around a bar. She begins to unscrew those two.

While holding the parts and tools for Marketa, Elliott reacts to a faint noise. A low toned croak followed by a strong buzzing sound. "Did anyone else hear that?" he asks.

"What did you hear?" asks Evzen.

"A croak with a buzz, two sounds that I don't like a combination of."

"Uh oh," the biologist says.

"What do you mean 'uh oh'? Don't say that and not give an explanation!" Elliott says anxiously.

"Well, one creature I know of that makes that particular noise is a fog stinger. A large bug that has legs meant for grasping large prey and a stinger meant for paralysis."

Everyone falls silent for several seconds, staring at Evzen for anything that might make their situation at least slightly better.

"Don't worry," Evzen says, chuckling nervously, "As long as we're not next to their hive we'll be fine."

"That is not comforting," Elliott says, on edge.

Radek watches Marketa work on the connecting rod while also keeping a lookout for anything hostile. The area is quiet. A little too quiet, Elliott thinks. The rest of the crew peers around, hoping nothing would show itself. But wouldn't we rather see it first rather than it hiding, he thinks. The questions and statements swim through Elliott's mind.

The only sounds coming from anywhere is the clanking and ratcheting from the replacing of the connecting rod. After a couple minutes, Marketa pulls out a handful of bolts and the two pieces of the severed rod to Elliott. The both of them switch, giving her the new rod to install.

The noise is there again, low croak and a buzz. This time it is louder, but still nothing appears in sight. The buzzing stops and the feeling of something watching increases significantly. Radek glances upwards to the top of the plane and there it is. A giant bug, the size of a human if not larger. The abdomen holding the thick stinger is long with black and brown stripes. Its thorax contains six slots that encase the legs when it hides them. Right now they are holding the roof of the plane. Its wings are in sets of three, standing on end which make it look bigger than normal. The last distinguishing feature is the compound eyes bulging with pixelated pupils.

It moves across the plane without making a sound, preparing a pounce. Its stinger throbs and the wings vibrate as it moves closer to Marketa. Just as it jumps for her, Radek moves in the way in time. The fog stinger, not expecting the sudden motion, wraps its legs around him and lifts him into the air.

Quickly thinking, Elliott releases Coil to go help him. As quickly as the fog stinger pounced, several more jump out from the mist. Close to a dozen fog stingers charge towards their prey. Chernak does not hesitate to shield his friends, flinging his tail to swat the bugs away. Eva pushes Evzen behind the dragon while pulling out a metal rod the size of her hand. Then with one click of a button, the rod transforms into a spear.

Chernak catches a bug in his mouth, crunching it in his mighty jaws that destroys the exoskeleton and spewing its yellow blood in the air. Two more attempt to pierce him with their stingers but are stopped by sharp claws and a thick head.

A set of legs grasps Elliott by the shoulders, lifting him up like Radek. He draws his pointed device from his wrist again to stab the bug through the face and upper thorax. It croaks and releases its grip, dropping Elliott about ten feet. He lands on his feet, dropping into a roll to suppress the force.

Radek flails around trying to escape the creature's grasp. Coil comes to the rescue with a spinning saw to cut through the legs. The natural reaction it takes is taking its stinger and pushing it into his shoulder before letting him go. He falls several feet, tumbling onto the ground with a thud.

"Radek!" Marketa calls.

"What!" Radek calls back. "It's too dark, I can't hear you that well!"

"You idiot! Get over here! Follow the noise!" she screams.

While fighting off her own assailant, Eva orders everyone to get back into the plane. A bug lunges at her, but she sees it coming. She drives the spear upward into the head, flipping it over her shoulder and ready for the next one.

Evzen opens the fuselage door to the passenger seats when a fog stinger tackles him to the ground. With his knowledge of the anatomy of these insects, he knows there is a pressure point where the thorax meets the head. While on the ground, Evzen waits for the foe to come closer until it is in punching distance. The fog stinger is completely above him, preparing for a paralysis strike when a sudden blow to its throat immobilizes the bug completely. It topples over to its side, scrunching its legs into its chest.

Elliott grabs Evzen's hand to help him up. "Nice one! But we have to get out of here, now! There are more that are swarming the plane!"

He is right, the fog stingers seem to be doubling in numbers every time one falls. Chernak still manages to take down multiple at a time, but even he begins to struggle against this army.

"HELP!" Marketa screams. The sudden cry causes all of their hearts to sink. Each one of them sprint in her direction, hoping nothing terrible has happened yet. Searching through the mist is tough, but the group manages to find Marketa batting away at a stinger with her hammer. Elliott tackles the creature to the ground, stabbing it with his vibrating point.

"He's hurt bad!" she screams, pointing at the lying body of Radek, who is writhing in pain.

"I got him!" Elliott says. "Just run away from the plane! We need to get out of here!"

None of them hesitate. They know if they stay long enough the swarm that has ambushed them would soon be able to have them for dinner. Elliott pulls Radek up by the sleeves on his shoulders. He bends down and lifts him up over his own shoulder with all his strength. He then follows the rest of the group away from Fiala.

"No!" Radek mutters, raising a hand towards his beloved Fiala.

"I'm sorry, but we have to!" Elliott says, breathing heavily.

The sound of buzzing begins to dissipate in the distance behind them. The plane disappears in an instant along with the swarm. Radek's eyes well up with tears as he watches the entire scene become lost in the Smoke Cloud. His shoulder hurts more than ever while it bounces up and down from Elliott dashing to catch up with the group. Then the sudden feeling of falling overwhelms the pain.

Elliott doesn't see the drop off ahead of him, causing him to slip and roll down a muddy cliffside. Shrubs, vines, roots, and rocks are the objects the two of them fall into. Finally they reach a bottom where the rest of the group seems to have fallen in the same space.

Lying in a marsh now, the mist no longer lingers around the

area. Most of what can be seen is swamp and marsh. The air is humid with a foul stench of decomposing plants and mud covered bugs. The trees are thick and a large quantity blocks any chance of seeing a horizon. There are only small portions in the canopy where light can squeeze through.

"No go back," Radek groans.

Elliott slowly rises up to face the fallen pilot. "We can't go back. It's too dangerous. I'm sorry but she's gone, we did what we could," he says.

"You called her 'she'," Radek says, quivering his lips. "But you still left her!" he says, now scrunching his face with anger. He starts breathing sporadically, hyperventilating through his mask.

Elliott quickly pulls off the mask from the straps. "Breath!" he says, trying to sit him up, pulling off his own mask.

"He's going into shock. We need to patch that wound," Eva says, grabbing a medical kit from her pack. She tears away the torn parts of his jacket with surprising strength. She takes a gauze patch to place on his shoulder, causing him to wince. "Elliott, I need you to pull him towards you for the other side."

The hunter grabs him by the waist and pulls Radek to his side. Eva quickly cleans away the mud and blood before patching it with another gauze pad.

Just as they place him back down, Marketa kneels down to him. "You–you saved me. You've never done that before," she says softly.

Straining from the patched wound he mutters, "It wasn't the craziest thing I've done," he chuckles.

"But it was the best thing you've done," Marketa says, her cheeks turning as red as her hair.

Then, Radek's face turns blank. His movement becomes still without a reaction of agony. No hint of expressions show across any part of his face. His muscles become still.

"No! Radek! Please don't die!" Marketa screams, beginning to sob.

"He's alright, Marketa," Evzen says. "He's becoming paralyzed. The toxins will wear off."

"Well then, while he's recovering we should start getting to Studeny Brazina. Going through the Swamp Mountains won't be easy," Eva says. "Evzen, do you have your map and compass?"

"Always do," he says, pulling out a roll of parchment and a device with a needle pointing just to their left. He looks on the map for the marked city on the map on the northern parts of the Swamp Mountains, orienting the compass to match it, and looks back up. "Studeny Brazina is that way," he says pointing in that general direction.

9

THE SWAMP'S WRATH

Muddy and muggy. That is what the Swamp Mountains mostly contain. Towering formations of rock with a thick blanket of muck and trees. Each step that the crew takes is another hole made into the moist overcoat waist-deep, hardly touching any stone beneath it. The redeeming factor is the amount of vines and branches hanging above them to hoist themselves up. Although, Chernak has no need for them since trudging through mud is a cakewalk, even with a paralyzed Radek lying on his back.

The smell of rotting fruits and plants never seems to go away. The smell only intensifies with a complimentary aroma of gunk left behind by all sorts of animals. Here it is better to see than the Smoke Cloud, however it still hinders some of the light from above.

The group has been trudging for several minutes in silence. At least among themselves they are quiet. The rest of the swamp never sounds at peace. Whipping sounds from a whipping finch as its mating call, hissing from a crossed frog as a warning, even howling from corroded wolves in the distance. Chirping, creaking, snarling, snapping, the swamp seems like the loudest place in Poclad.

Marketa takes another look back at Radek, who is still blank faced. "I hope he'll be alright. How long until the toxins wear off?" she says.

"I'm not entirely sure. It could be hours, even days if it's bad enough. It could be any minute now if he's lucky," Evzen says.

"Most importantly, he's going to be fine. As long as he's still breathing and we keep an eye on him he'll start moving again," Eva reassures.

Marketa takes a deep breath to release some tension. Eva, who walks sidelong Elliott, says to him, "Thank you for saving him. It means a lot not only to me but to them as well."

"Well," he says, "I know how important you all are to each other. It's the same thing I feel with Chernak and Coil. I guess some things are more important than treasure," Elliott says.

She smiles, biting her bottom lip subconsciously. The group continues to hike without saying a word for several more minutes. The mud gradually grows thinner, the depth going up to their knees. The further they go the more it feels like they travel in a circle, even though they are sure they are going in a straight line.

"Marketa," Evzen says, "You have a sucker."

The mechanic searches her body and notices a builder leech on her thigh. A worm-like creature that is dark blue in color with multiple large pores that are used for other leeches to stack on top of each other. Marketa swipes it off with ease, paying almost no mind to it.

"Could you check me, Elliott," Evzen asks, turning his back to him.

Checking the biologist's back, Elliott notices dozens of leeches building on him making a peculiar shape like a pentagon. He almost flinches at the sight of them, not expecting so many. The dragon rider swipes them off with his hands, showering them in the mud.

But there is something else he notices as he looks down at the leeches. A vine moves towards Evzen's ankle, slithering like a snake.

"Evzen move!" Elliott says, pushing him out of the way. But as quickly as they move, so does the vine and there appears to be more.

The plants entangle the two of them, lifting them in the air. Once the rest of the crew begin to move in to help, they become entangled as well. The strength of the vines is unmatched as it lifts Chernak into the air, preventing any further movement. In fact, the more they move, so does the plant.

Everyone now flails around, using every bit of energy to get loose. But no matter how hard they try they are no match for vines that grapple them as tight as rope. Elliott and the rest can't move their limbs to grab any sharp object to cut them loose. Chernak attempts to bite and claw but even he can't move very far. Coil has been sealed shut by the vines, preventing him from using any tools. He can only mutter a high pitched zooming noise.

"Wait a minute," Evzen says, slowing his movement. "This is uchopeni vine."

"This is one of those times where we actually want you to explain something, Evzen!" Eva says.

"It's a motion sensing vine, the more you move the faster it'll grapple and eat you."

"I'll say!" Elliott says as the vines take him to what looks like a large opening in its main stem acting as a mouth. The top of it is brown with dark spots that open like a lid. Inside is a bright gelatinous filled halfway up the stem taking a nectar-yellow color. Elliott's head is now dipped into the mouth while he tries desperately to get loose.

"Everyone stop moving!" Evzen screams.

The mere crew stops writhing, not moving a single muscle. Once they do, the vines stop in their tracks as well. Elliott's head stays in the gaping mouth of the uchopeni, holding his breath. Everyone is suspending above the ground, the vines still not letting their grip give.

"Alright," Evzen says, "Can anyone produce some sort of a flame?"

The crew, thinking the exact same thing, peers over towards Chernak. The dragon takes notice of everyone's gaze. *Oh because I'm a dragon I should be able to breathe fire, right?* He snarls, but no one seems to understand him.

"There should be a lighter in my pack," Eva says. "Marketa, can you reach it?"

"I can but if I move the vines will move too."

"As long as you move very slowly, you should be fine," Evzen instructs.

Carefully, Marketa reaches towards Eva's pack. The vines move at the same speed as her, but do not pull with the same strength. Stretching as far as she can, the mechanic manages to reach the zipper of the leader's pack. She opens it, beginning to dig through the contents in her pack.

"It should be in the shape of a flare," Eva says.

Finally, Marketa pulls out a red hilt with a black hood at the top where the fire comes out. She zips the pack back up and quickly finds the button to activate the fuse. A spark pops out followed by an orange burning flame about four inches tall. Immediately feeling the intense heat of the lighter, the plant slithers away and completely loses grip with everyone nearby.

It drops Marketa, Eva, and Evzen, but Marketa must hold the lighter up closer to Chernak and Elliott, who is still about to be eaten. Once the fire comes close to them, the vines soon drop the hunter, the dragon, and the robot. The rest of them drop into the mud again.

Elliott stands up while whipping off mud from his face. "That was embarrassing. We don't talk about that, nobody thinks about that. You got it?" he says, irritated.

The crew stares at him smirking, doing their best to hold back laughter.

I'll remember it. Chernak huffs and puffs.

Elliott scoffs, "You don't get treats."

You didn't give me the ones you promised yesterday. He whines.

"There you go, it cancels out. That worked out perfectly," he says in a sarcastic tone.

The group moves along, now more cautious of any plant life that makes the slightest nudge. The amount of trees around them begin to dwindle when they encounter more clearings and ponds. Small ripples in the water can be seen and roots on the edges wiggle, possibly due to an animal underwater. A light fog rests over them, not blocking too much vision but enough to set the crew on edge.

Then suddenly, a loud voice comes from the direction of Chernak. "I'm hungry!" is what breaks the silence, causing everyone in the group to jump and scream in succession. "My stomach is empty and my heart is empty! I want to go back to Fiala now!"

Radek is talking while resting on Chernak's saddle but doesn't move any other part of his body. Just his mouth and eyes, which is all he needs.

"You screeching toad! I almost fainted!" Marketa screams.

"And I almost died, it was pretty fun actually. But I'm still angry you left her! All of you! And now I'm hungry!" he complains.

"Most of the rations were in the plane. We can eat when we get to Studeny Brazina. How much further, Evzen?" Eva says.

"Hard to tell. My guess is that we will either get there in the next couple of hours or even in a couple days."

"Really?" Elliott says, "That's your guess? That's a wide range, don't you think?"

"Well I can't tell of any markers right now since we're in the middle of the swamp. We could be here," Evzen says, pointing at the top portion between the Smoke Cloud and the Swamp Mountains. "Or we could be here on the bottom where we came out of the Smoke Cloud. What I do know is that we are going northeast, so that we can either find the edge of the continent and follow it northward. Or we can stumble upon the city by accident and avoid the Burning Iceland."

The crew nod their heads in understanding, now realizing what kind of situation they were in. Radek, on the other hand, doesn't seem to be listening. "So what part of the plan says we're going back?"

Eva sighs heavily. "Look, Radek, we can't worry about Fiala right now. The only thing we need to focus on is getting to a safe place. Now you may not like that, but you're dealing with it, no questions asked."

Elliott gets a small shiver down his spine after hearing that. He can't tell if he is blushing or if it's just hot and he's sweating. It could be both, but after her words sunk into Radek he stops talking. That's the first time I've seen him shut up, he thinks. Besides the paralysis of course.

Coil hovers towards Radek's face, making a happy zip sound showing his relief for him. As they continue, the light fog grows thicker. Oddly enough, the sounds of swamp creatures become dimmer. So dim that they almost cannot be heard. The ground turns into a slight downwards incline.

Everything falls completely silent all of a sudden. The crew stops in their tracks.

"Anyone else getting a funny feeling?" Elliott asks.

Suddenly something moves beneath them, causing each member to slip down the path that leads to a much steeper hill. Radek is flown off the saddle, falling in Elliott's direction towards the left. Chernak and Coil catch themselves by flying above while the rest of the crew falls towards the right.

The slope is slick, with nothing to hold onto. Elliott just tumbles down into the fog that hovers above the lower parts of the swamp. It never seems to end, one of the astounding features of the Swamp Mountains is the number of steep slopes one can stumble upon.

Tossing and turning until finally Elliott comes to a stop onto his back where immense pressure and pain ensue. The agony is enough to hold him in place, stiffening his muscle. That is until the sound of bubbling in water nearby catches his attention. Straining to roll off to his side, Elliott tilts his head up to see what the noise could be. The realization quickly takes over when he sees Radek with his face submerged in the muddy water.

He turns the paralyzed body over to allow Radek to take in a huge gasp of air. As soon as he coughs, spits, and fills his lungs with air, his first words are, "I want my plane."

"Why don't you walk over there and get it?" Elliott says sarcastically.

Radek just laughs. "That's funny, you're laughing at my heroic condition."

Ignoring him, Elliott calls out to anyone from the crew, but even if they heard him there is not a single answer from them. No person, dragon, or robot in sight. The only thing that is within earshot is Radek's mumbling. He is quiet but the only words Elliott can decipher are 'Fiala', 'love', and 'go back'.

The young hunter grunts in rage and pain from the fall. "Serpent's crystals," he says under his breath. "Why me?" He then heaves Radek's arms over his shoulders and stands up. "We have to go find the others. I don't care how much you complain. We have to move."

"If you say so! I have a lot of complaining in the tank," Radek says.

Oh great, Elliott thinks. He pulls Radek on his back and they continue through the swamp past the small pond. The trees they pass are stinking birch that are gray in color with black stripes. The stripes are sacks full of sap that are commonly used for sauces and glazes.

Radek, who tries moving his head, chomps his teeth towards the closest tree but can't quite get close enough. After missing his chance, he pouts and continues to share his grievance.

———

"Is everyone alright?" Eva asks, searching around grass, weeds, and brush.

"I think I landed on my toolbox," Marketa says, sprawled on the ground further away from her.

The woods here are full of tall grass mixed with spiny leaves. Some plants are wider and taller than others with a thick stem. The air is significantly warmer and moist like a sauna. Sweat quickly drips from Eva's head and dew lingers on each leaf.

"We have to move. We need to find the others," Eva demands.

"We should not move at all," Evzen says on the other side of Eva.

The bushes rustle and the sound of bark creaking renders the girls speechless and still. Something slithers through the ground, the light coming from above the treeline dims as several large leaves create a dome around them.

"This is absolutely fascinating!" Evzen says.

"Wh–what is fascinating, Evzen?" Eva says, still unmoved.

"Only a couple people have ever seen this creature before. It's quite amazing that we found one."

"Evzen! What did we find? You're making me nervous!" Marketa says, beginning to tremble.

Then the creature reveals itself. An incredibly large stem for a body with red spines all over. Eight vine-like limbs protrude from its body that spread throughout the area. The legs look like roots that shuffle through the dirt beneath them. The head is much like a serpent with a horned snout, its eyes resemble the red petals it forms on its arms. The teeth are the most frightening, each row hanging out of its mouth like tusks but only sharper and finely tuned.

"It's an Anilantae! A creature that possesses the properties of both a plant and an animal. The creature contains cells with both centrosomes and cell walls as well as chloroplasts. I've always wanted to encounter one! We must've landed in its nest," Evzen geeks out.

"Great, now you've seen one. I think it would be best to get out of its nest, don't you think?" Eva says.

Evzen laughs nervously. "Well, we should've moved earlier. Because now she's trapped us in here with her rapid overgrowth."

The two girls glare at him with furious looks. "So you've been gawking about the anilantae this whole time, explaining what it is and how fascinating it is, and you didn't once stop to think that we should do something about it first?" Eva says, building up with fury.

"You even told us to stop moving!" Marketa says, trying to contain her anger.

The vine-like arms begin to slither around each individual, creating a barrier of thorns and spines. Marketa presses on her belt buckle that releases guards on her legs and arms.

"Oh by the way, don't touch those spines. They'll release a fatal toxin to anyone," Evzen warns.

"We need to have you practice warning on time!" Marketa mentions.

═══

After hovering over the fog for a few minutes, Chernak and Coil land into the wetlands below. The two of them trek through the swamp in search of their master or anyone from the crew. Coil frantically flies around Chernak's head, making worried stuttering zip sounds almost like he wonders if the worst has happened to them.

I'm sure they're fine. Chernak snarls, irritated by the repetitive circles Coil makes.

As if it couldn't get more annoying, the little robot jumps up and down through the air looking like he might explode at some point.

Calm down. The dragon growls.

Pretty soon, Coil shudders and swiftly darts around the air without any sense of restraint.

Chernak roars to get the frantic robot to stop, scaring him so much he might as well have loosened a couple bolts. After the sudden shock, Coil turns to a tree to quiver like he is crying, followed by low toned zip noises.

The annoyed beast, now feeling some slight guilt, grunts and walks sidelong Coil. *Look, I didn't mean to lose my cool. Just quit your crying and help me find Elliott, alright?*

The emotional machine turns to Chernak, nodding in understanding while he wipes away imaginary tears from his face.

You know you have nothing on your face, right? Chernak snorts.

Then the two of them hear the sound of someone talking up ahead. Thinking the same thing, both of them sprint for the noise.

"Not once did any of them show a sliver of respect to her. They probably think it's good that we left her behind, as if she doesn't have any feelings. She carries us to every hunt we go on. Did you know Marketa threw a wrench at Fiala? She was aiming for me, but she still hurt her and didn't even say sorry!" Radek's rants don't seem to end. The few minutes of walking just feels like several hours.

"Yeah . . . sure," Elliott says, never having to hold back so much irritation in his life.

"I remember when she was built," Radek sighs. "Her wings were so shiny, the cockpit was so beautiful. It was the one thing I was really good at. I didn't have to scrap for food as long as I was the one taking everyone places. But now she's gone! And now I have no use for this group whatsoever! Just leave me! Let me sink into the mud! Let the bugs eat me! No! Let the mushrooms take me! The bugs are too good for me! Leave me!"

Elliott growls, throwing himself and Radek onto the ground. "As much as I want to leave you here, Radek, I can't! I'm sorry you lost your precious plane. I get that you have a connection to it, and to be brutally honest it is quite irritatingly strong," He yells. The hunter takes in a big breath of air and releases it slowly. "What I also have to be honest about is that the plane didn't have value until you brought it to her. If it wasn't for you, you guys wouldn't have accomplished so much. It would've taken so much longer to get from one place to another. So stop sulking about the plane and let's get out of here and worry about her later."

Stunned by his words, Radek now cannot come up with another complaint. Now that Elliott is satisfied that the words got to him, he picks up Radek again to continue their search. Once he is on Elliott's back, the two of them hear rustling in the trees. Something large was making its way through the swamp at a fast pace.

Not able to react quick enough, Elliott and Radek are struck down by Chernak's massive body. The dragon loses his balance, causing him to tumble with the rest of them into a small area full of brush.

The paralyzed pilot flies a little further in the brush just in front of a very disturbing creature. "Someone might have to check my pants later, I can't feel anything but I know what my body wants to do," Radek says, as the anilantae growls through its finely sharpened teeth.

"About time you showed up. Do you think your dragon can do something about our situation?" Eva asks, avoiding the pointed vines.

"First I'd like to know what situation this is," Elliott says, slowly rising from the impact.

"Yeah, Evzen, could you please tell me what that is," Radek says, still sprawled on the ground beneath it.

"It's called an anilantae, something you should be very afraid of right now," Evzen explains.

"Oh ok," he says. The pilot takes a second to take in the situation before he screams bloody murder at the sight of the monster opening its mouth to prepare to chomp.

Chernak snatches Radek before the anilantae could get to him. Elliott quickly uses his vibrating point to slice through the vines surrounding his friends. Each cut causes the creature to roar. As soon as everyone has an opening they dart out of the area.

Each person forces their way through bushes, weeds, and vines. The anilantae uproots anything in its path with the monstrous legs kicking up dirt and mud. Bark breaks from the body of the beast scraping against it. Every obstacle in its way is severed, bent, or otherwise destroyed. Nothing seems to stop it anytime soon.

"Chernak, fly! Do something! Isn't that what a dragon does?" Radek yells.

But Chernak cannot hear him. The anilantae sabotages so much vegetation it creates a large pathway behind it. The further they go the closer the monster gets to the party. It just comes into Radek's reach as it roars, causing him to scream in absolute fear.

Just as it reaches for him and Chernak, they break through the last bit of swamp and into the outskirts of a city wall. The wooden gates are left wide open and the gang dives for it. The sound of the anilantae dissipates, indicating that it gave up and began to return to its nest.

Everyone gasps for air, lying on the floor with relief filling their souls. The pain from every fall and impact begins to set into Elliott, aching from the neck and down.

Then, Radek's hands shoot up in the air as he screams, "Let's do that again!"

1∅

SAVING FIALA

Studeny Brazina is a city mostly made from wood and stone due to the nearby Swamp Mountains. The layout of the city is much more organized than any of the others in Poclad. The walls surround the town in a large square with wooden turrets on each corner. The buildings making up the town are mostly log cabins with chimneys producing smoke, which gives the scent of assorted spices and burning wood. The streets are gravel pavement outlined with neatly cut bricks.

Each house is beautifully decorated with pots full of flowers, trimmed vines sticking to the sides, and sanded down logs. The citizens walking around wear quite light clothing, with the men either wearing a linen shirt or not a shirt at all with baggy work shorts. The women wear a light long sleeve that typically reaches down to the belly button and work shorts identical to the men.

The town is a main source of lumber, food, and stonework. Certain huts hang signs for smiths and basket weavers. The centerpiece of the city is a larger cabin that is the tavern where tree houses sit around it on top of small trees.

The people of this city stare as they watch the Mere crew walk towards the tavern. Double doors are what they open towards the tavern, where they see several filled tables, chairs, and a bar in the back. All conversation inside stops when the crew walk in, smelling of rotting plants and covered in mud.

"There's a weed that needs to be cut down outside," Elliott comments to break the silence. "It's pretty big, and mean."

But the people inside stay silent except for one guy in the back that coughs, then the rest of them go back to their drinks and food. Each member leaves a boot print of mud and drips with sweat. Eva pays for everyone in the group for food and drinks, mostly to calm down Radek who is literally twitching as he waits for his food.

Their food reaches the table, neatly prepped, steaming, and seasoned. The group spares no time in stuffing their faces. Elliott tosses Chernak's food out the window for him to feast upon.

"So what's the plan now?" Elliott asks after devouring his food.

Eva shrugs her shoulders. "It looks like we're going to have to continue by foot."

"NO! We have to go back!" Radek screams immediately.

"Radek, there's no way to get back. The plane is gone. We can't get to it through that cloud," she says.

"Well," Marketa interrupts. "That's not entirely true. I

made a compass specially made for a situation like this. It pinpoints the exact location of Fiala through a micro tracker."

"And that is why I love you!" Radek says, giving Marketa a quick kiss on the cheek, causing her to blush severely.

"But even then, you'll still be surrounded by fog stingers. How will you get past them?" Evzen asks.

"I don't know. But I'm going to get my baby with or without you," he says, crossing his arms that indicates that his decision is final.

Everyone falls silent, waiting for anyone to protest against him. Eva, realizing that she won't be able to change his mind, turns to Elliott. While drinking his cold beverage in a clay mug, he catches her eyeing him.

Immediately Elliott shakes his head, "No. Nope. I'm good."

But Eva tilts her head slightly, giving him a smirk. "No, it's not happening. I have done enough," Elliott refuses.

Her eyes, her beautiful blue eyes, continue to be fixed onto his. Her face is something to both be captivated by and intimidated by. Submission slowly shrouds around Elliott. He groans, scrunches his face, clenches his fists, and finally says, "Serpent's crystals," as he stands up. "Fine. Radek, come with Chernak and I. Everyone else stays here. It'll be a quick trip."

"YAY! I love you, Elliott! Truly!" Radek says, raising his arms in the air for a hug and quickly embracing him before he can react.

"Yeah yeah yeah, don't mention it. Truly, just don't," Elliott says, kindly pushing him away.

"Before you go," Marketa says, "I still haven't screwed in the rod all the way. You need to secure it before you can fly."

She digs through her toolbox to pull out two bolts and her trusty wrench. Very reluctantly, she hands the pieces to Elliott. "Just please be careful how you reattach it," she says, tensing her shoulders.

"Don't worry," Elliott reassures. "Think of it as my trial run as your student." That seemed to calm her down some.

"So what's the plan?" Radek asks, now jumping up and down. "Are we going to fight off these bugs with fire? Can I use Eva's spear?" Eva has a physical reaction after that last part, refusing to have him touch her beloved weapon.

"Relax," the dragon rider says. "We're going to dig under the ground with Chernak. Once the compass says we're close enough, we'll sneak up to fix the plane and head out. So bring your mask and I'll need that compass."

Marketa hands over the device, which is a clear sphere with a blue needle pointing south west. The two of them walk out towards Chernak, who is waiting patiently with Coil.

I don't like the look that you have. Chernak seems to say.

"I still look better than you," Elliott retorts, which causes Chernak to growl. "We're going back to the Smoke Cloud and getting that plane back."

The dragon snorts a puff of air in his face. *Why the hell would you go back?*

"Because I have to. Radek won't stop talking about it until he gets it back. So get ready for a dig."

The crew come out to wish them luck. Marketa especially comes to Radek to give him a long hug, telling him to be careful. Eva looks over to Elliott and says, "Please take care of him."

Elliott nods, "I promise," he says, giving her a reassuring smile.

Elliott and Radek prepare for their flight. The pilot grabs his gas mask and straps his gloves onto his hands. Elliott leaps onto Chernak, offering a hand to Radek who eagerly grabs it to be lifted onto the back of the saddle. The dragon launches into the air after his rider yanks on the reins.

The Swamp Mountains are much more clear in the air. Towering pillars of rock covered in marsh cascade around this region. Below the mountains seems like a jungle, trees upon trees leave no chance at seeing the ground. Fog sits like a blanket in multiple areas, including the space the crew once fell. To their left is more swamp and then a dropoff into a vast ocean, indicating the edge of the continent. To their right is the Smoke Cloud which still gives an ominous feeling down their spine.

"Hey, Chernak," Elliott says, showing a malicious smirk. "How about we show Radek what it's like to fly our way?"

I was waiting for you to ask that. Chernak seems to say.

Without warning, the dragon rolls over to take a deep nose dive towards the swamp below. By pure instinct, Radek grips onto Elliott's shoulder and stomach while he blurts out a scream of initial terror that slowly turns into excitement. Just before they hit the treeline, Elliott pulls up to level out.

Then a quick turn made by Chernak goes towards the nearest mountain. He soars along the side, so close Radek is able to stick out his hand to skid across the mud. Chernak increases in altitude to create a spiral around the mountain until they reach the top where they spin out towards the Smoke Cloud again.

"Nothing will beat Fiala's flying, but I've never done that before!" Radek says. "Thank you for helping her out."

"Don't thank me yet," Elliott says. "We have to actually get her out of that cloud. Now, you get in front of me so that when we go under you won't be hit by any debris."

Radek obeys, slowly switching seats with Elliott. The two of them shift carefully but eventually succeed. As they come closer to the Smoke Cloud, Chernak begins descending at an incline towards the ground.

"Now lean forward and to your left, Chernak's horns will protect you," Elliott says.

Again, the pilot obeys. Now with his weight moving to the left, Elliott has room for himself to lean into the saddle and to the right. He pulls his mask on and Radek slips on his. Once the two of them are ready, Elliott yells, "Dig, Chernak!"

The dragon plunges into the ground, creating a gaping hole in the sediment. The soft mud quickly turns into rough stone flying past them. But no matter what, Chernak's sharp wings, large claws, and drill-shaped head continue to cut through like paper. The grinding on rock and smashing of rubble is all that can be heard.

Elliott takes the compass out of his pocket to see how close they are. The needle still points south west but it begins to point upward. He tugs up on the reins a little to tell Chernak to move that direction.

Then suddenly, the dirt around them vanishes. What Chernak enters is extremely sinister. The surface is not what they see but a cavern that seems several hundred feet in diameter with green and yellow walls with sap-like textures. Webs of this material center into one large sphere where hundreds of fog stingers buzz around. The entire area is dimly lit by biolu-minescent nectar around the spherical web.

"I think we found the source of our bug problem," Elliott says. He looks at the compass again which is now pointing straight up. "Let's move before they attack."

Chernak flaps his wings harder to rise into the ceiling that he attempts to break through. As soon as he touches the ceiling, the texture reveals itself as a gelatinous layer that traps Chernak before he can reach the rock. The sudden stop of force throws Elliott and Radek off the saddle and into the gelatinous material. It acts like glue, immobilizing completely.

"Well that's not good," Elliott says.

"It tastes good though," Radek says, licking the glue and taking bites out of it.

Elliott rolls his eyes. "Cut that out, we need to get out of here."

The stingers buzz around, noticing a hole in their home and looking for the source. Chernak kicks and claws trying to break through the layer of glue. He makes progress but still struggles to make his way to the rock. While he works to get his companions out, the other two hang by the glue while they watch the bugs in the center work on their home.

Most of the stingers fly around for the source of the disturbance while some carry larvae and nectar. The spherical web is translucent and in between the webs is a large queen that has a pulsating thorax. That's something I would like to avoid, Elliott thinks.

"Looks like there's a patrol! I can't get caught again!" Radek says, beginning to squirm.

He is right that the fog stingers are searching the area and crawling closer towards them along the walls.

"Chernak, can you dig any faster?" Elliott asks, worrisome.

Just a second, I'm grabbing a snack. What do you think I've been doing? The dragon grunts.

"Oh man!" Radek panics. "They've had a taste of me and now they want seconds! Tell Fiala I love her but she can't have another husband!"

"Shut your idiotic mouth, Radek! If you start panicking they will find us. Chernak will get us out soon."

Chernak pries open the gelatinous to finally reach the stone above. Now he bangs his face into it to start making a hole. Dust and rubble fall from the ceiling, which causes the fog stingers below to become aware of their location. The stingers screech to alert the others who fly as quickly as they can towards the intruders.

"Chernak! A little faster!" Elliott says.

The dragon pushes through the stone to make a gap. He turns to snatch Radek first who is tensing his muscles to the point where it hurts. Radek grabs hold of the saddle while Chernak pulls Elliott out. The dragon jumps down and flaps his wings to build momentum. Just before the bugs reach them, Elliott and Radek lean forward and Chernak is cutting through the stone again. Tons of debris fall behind them knocking the stingers back into their home.

Soon enough, they reach the surface, nearly hitting Fiala on the way up. Nothing has changed since the last time they were there, at least nothing that they can see. The plane doesn't seem to have any significant scratches done to her. It appears as if she hasn't moved at all.

Chernak lands and the two passengers jump off to head for Fiala. Radek immediately embraces the haul, trying to kiss it through the mask. Elliott heads for the hatch leading to the engine. The connecting wire is still intact, hanging loose by two bolts.

Elliott turns to Chernak, "Keep the bugs busy while I work on this. Don't let them come through there," he says pointing at the hole they exited from.

The ground beneath them rumbles from the amount of angry bug wings flapping about to squeeze through the ground. Chernak prepares his claws and teeth for anything that comes out of there. Radek hops into the plane, waiting for Elliott to finish his work.

Elliott anxiously begins screwing one bolt in. The motion is harder than it looks, having to avoid smashing against the piston or any other wiring within the engine. The ratcheting of the wrench is overheard by the crawling and buzzing of the stingers coming from beneath them.

Finally the first bolt is in and Elliott nearly drops the next one while pulling it out of his pocket. Some of the stingers have made their way up to the surface. But instead of breathing in the air of the Smoke Cloud, they are met with a mighty jaw chomping down on them. Or a claw slashing against them, cracking the exoskeleton and rupturing joints.

While tightening the last bolt, Elliott notices a fog stinger that has slipped by Chernak. The next target it looks for comes into its sights. It turns towards Elliott and charges for him. He turns the wrench faster, faster, as fast as he can. Just before the stinger reaches him, it is met with a massive swing of a wrench that knocks it to the ground and breaks its neck.

Elliott closes the hatch and bangs on the haul to tell Radek to start the engine. He turns the master key, evens out the throttle, and turns the fuel pump on. The plane grumbles, wheezes, and dies out. Radek tries over again but it doesn't seem to work. The propeller seems to be stuck, grinding on something.

The young hunter grunts in anger. Elliott dashes to the propeller to observe what is going on. Unfortunately nothing becomes visible that is disrupting the plane. Thinking swiftly, Elliott grabs the blade of the propeller and yanks it down with all his strength. The blades spin, causing a piece of a stinger that was stuck inside flies out.

The blades spin normally, revving the engine beautifully. Satisfied that it works, Elliott runs towards the fuselage door but is suddenly pinned down onto his back. The sharp stinger rises and falls to pierce him. The hunter blocks the weapon with his foot, stopping just short of his pants. The bug's head reveals its pincers for a mouth, thrusting towards its prey's face. Dodging, pushing, and squirming to break free, Elliott does everything he can to avoid being eaten.

As quick as he was put onto the ground, the fog stinger is knocked off by a swift swing of a wrench. Radek stands above him with a hand extended. "That makes two today," he says.

Elliott takes the hand, standing up to see Chernak having to back off from the hole. "I think that's our que! Get in the plane! Let's get out of here!" Elliott demands.

Radek climbs into the cockpit and gives power through the throttle to make the plane go forward. Chernak soars toward Elliott, who is running in the direction of the plane. Just before the dragon reaches him, Elliott jumps into the saddle, puts his feet in the stirrups, and takes the reins to follow Fiala.

The swarm attempts to grab hold of the plane. Some of them

are chopped into smithereens from the blades of the propeller. Others are able to latch onto the wings and windshield. Elliott takes Chernak to come closer to the plane to swat the bugs off. On the wings, the dragon whacks them with his tail and moves to the windshield. He chomps onto the head of the fog stinger, shaking it away.

"Come on, baby! Climb! Climb!" Radek says, pulling on the wheel to angle the plane up. The plane lifts into the air.

Without any more pursuers, the plane and the dragon emerge from the Smoke Cloud. Radek cheers in triumph and sighs with relief that he is back in his favorite spot in the whole world. The city of Studeny Brazina is not too far past the muddy mountains ahead in the evening light. They take no time to goof off and only focus on reaching the city without another scratch. Elliott removes his mask to breathe in the fresh air.

"I won't lie to you buddy, I kinda miss that jagged plane," Elliott says.

Eh, I've seen fish that could fly better. Chernak snarls.

"What fish have you seen that flies?"

The ones that fly into my mouth. The dragon huffs and puffs.

Elliott shakes his head but can't help but laugh out loud.

Radek descends into a clear space of grass and ice just outside of the city. The sound of the plane can be heard for miles and causes the rest of the crew to dart outside. Seeing that Fiala is back in the air, the three of them and Coil cheer with complete joy. Fiala has no trouble with the ground below her. The landing gear rolls with the speed of the plane perfectly. She slows down just shy of the walls where people inside are left wondering where the vehicle came from.

Once the plane lands, Radek steps out of the fuselage, raising his hands in the air to say, "Who's ready to continue our
adventure?"

11

THE BURNING ICE ROAD

"It was insane! We dug underground and found the hive and they were like bzzzzzz!" Radek says, making clawing hand gestures with his sound effects. "And then we got stuck in this glue! Then we fixed Fiala and she sensed my presence and started purring again! And then Elliott was like 'AHHH!' and I saved him!"

As the sky begins to turn dark, Radek cannot stop exaggerating the story of recovering the plane. Elliott rolls his eyes but chuckles with the group listening to what had happened. The landing area they chose is past the swamp and outside Studeny Brazina. An area of mostly grass that feeds into the frosty land of the Burning Iceland up ahead. There the group can see a vast land of ice with steam rising from multiple portions of the ground.

"Alright you kids," Eva laughs. "Let's get some sleep before going out tomorrow."

Radek opens his mouth to say something but Eva stops him before a word could come out. "Yes you can sleep in the plane," she says.

Elliott walks with her while the rest of the group race for the entrance. She walks close to him, nearly touching hands. "Thank you for watching him," she says softly.

Elliott shrugs, "It was nothing. If anything he was taking care of me. I hate to admit it but he did save my life."

"So you did scream like a little girl," she teases.

His face flushes with red. "I did not scream! I was pinned down in the heat of battle! Radek just happened to be there at the right time!" he defends.

But Eva just laughs. "It's alright, you're secret safe with me. We all get scared in the moment."

The young hunter just grunts while the leader smiles at his embarrassment. The two of them enter the city again, heading for the inn to find rooms to stay at. Elliott offers to pay for the rooms, each person having their own. Just before they get ready for bed, Eva gives Elliott a kiss on the cheek. He becomes flabbergasted, unmoving until she closes her door. He then goes to his room joyously awaiting the next day.

═══

While sleeping in the comfiest bed he has ever slept on, Elliott wakes up to the sound of banging on a door outside. But not his door, someone in the hallway of the inn is knocking on another door.

"Wake up! That treasure won't capture itself! Wake up, Mere Crew! Wake up!" Radek says, his voice very distinct.

The wondrous slumber quickly turns into an irritating awakening. His sore muscles force him to crawl out of bed and angrily open the door. Radek continues to bang on the door two rooms down. The rest of the crew on the other side of the hallway open their doors to the same sound. The excited pilot does not seem to notice.

"Radek!" everyone says synchronously.

The banging stops and Radek jumps, startled from the sudden name call. "Oh," he says, laughing nervously. "Are you guys ready?"

"I'll kill you," Marketa says groggily.

"I didn't hear him, what did he say?" Evzen says, rubbing his eyes.

"Clean up, you guys," Eva says, "We have a big day. We're almost there. Get all of your gear, eat, and let's head out."

The crew groans in understanding, each returning to their rooms to prepare for the day. After dressing and packing, the group grabs a quick breakfast consisting of eggs, vegetables, and fruit from the swamp. Some of the food is an acquired taste, most of the flavors being earthy. Marketa doesn't like some of it so she leaves it to Radek to finish the plate.

With food in their stomachs and energy built up inside, they head back to the plane to prepare for the next part of their journey. Radek hurries people on board as he is eager to get the day started.

Elliott takes one look at the plane and then back at Chernak. "I think I'll take another ride with them, is that alright with you?" he says.

The dragon looks at the plane then back at his friend and snorts. *Eh I don't care. But you owe me double treats afterwards.*

Elliott laughs. "It's a deal. Once we get that treasure I'll be able to buy you more than double treats." He then rushes over towards the plane before they close the fuselage door. Eva nearly shuts it until he grabs her attention. "I hope it's alright if I come along again," he says.

A big smile forms across her face and nods assurance that he can come aboard. He climbs in to see Evzen and Marketa with cheerful faces.

"I knew you'd come back," Evzen says with open arms.

Elliott shrugs. "I wanted to have one last crack at it," he says, taking a seat alongside Evzen.

"If you're not riding Chernak, can I have a crack at it?" Evzen asks eagerly.

Elliott laughs. "Not without me. Not that I don't trust you, it's that I don't trust him as much."

"Alright!" Radek announces. "Where to, boss?"

"I want to get as close as possible to Mount Spiral," Eva says. "We need a place to land in the Burning Iceland that's flat enough to drop us off and enough runway for you to take off. Mount Spiral doesn't have any places for you to land. After that, Evzen can use the waypoint to guide us to the treasure."

"I hear you. Let's fly!" the pilot says, starting up the plane.

"By the way," Elliott says to Evzen. "How far are we from the treasure?"

The cartographer pulls out the blue handheld radar device. He zooms out for the map of Poclad and a point on it can be seen in the center of a spiral landmass on the corner of the map. "We don't have much further. Once we land it should be a few days walk around the mountain range. It looks like wherever the Colossal Tooth is it has to be somewhere in the cavern, which is where the point is indicating," Evzen explains, making a long sigh.

"What's wrong?" Elliott asks.

"Nothing . . . it's just . . . most people don't come out alive."

Elliott scoots closer across the walkway and lays a hand on his shoulder. "Don't worry, we're going to make it out. Where's that optimism you always have?"

That seems to cheer him up significantly. "You're right. I can already see everyone cheering for us once we come back!"

"There you go," Elliott says, sitting back and buckling himself up for another plane ride.

Radek feeds energy through the throttle, the plane picks up speed through the icy grass. Sleet shoots up from the landing gear skidding across the grass. The nose rises and the plane lifts into the air, where the rest of the Burning Iceland can be seen much more clearly.

This piece of land is more of a massive glacier. This pack of ice is in between the Metallic Plains and Mount Spiral. Many parts of the glacier are steaming due to the magma that flows beneath it from Mount Iris. The reason it is called the Burning Iceland is because the ice never truly melts. The magma shifts the ice but it never goes away because of a peculiar phenomenon where the magma burns the ice beneath and it instantly freezes afterwards.

Mount Iris can be seen towards the west, erupting tons of molten iridium. The plains around it are completely covered in the metal that have created hills all over. Several mining facilities are set up around the Metallic Plains that have hardly made a dent in the region, like having an infinite source of money.

To the east is the pointy Mount Spiral, a mountain range

with steep and thin columns of rock like massive stalagmites. This corner of the continent has formed a large spiral, giving it the iconic name Mount Spiral.

"Such a beautiful view," Eva says, peering out the window facing the volcano.

"It really is," Elliott responds, looking in the same direction but mainly taking a peak towards Eva's beautiful face. Then he realizes something. "Hey, Evzen. Are we allowed to land in the Burning Iceland even though there's not a city?"

"As long as we don't disrupt an environment it's alright," he says. "Since it's all ice and shifting we're not disrupting much."

"Speaking of landing," Radek interrupts. "It'll be a bumpy ride when we get there. And I say that, because we're doing it exactly now." Then the plane is suddenly forced downwards.

All the passengers lift in their seats, their stomachs rising even higher. Elliott's instincts kick in by grabbing his own seat and ceiling. His gag reflexes begin to activate but he forces it back down. The ice below them gains closer and closer until Radek pulls up, suddenly bringing Fiala level to the ground.

The landing gear shears the ice beneath it, causing everyone to bounce as they touch the ground. But there doesn't seem to be much slowing down, not as much friction is holding the plane back. Radek puts the full weight of the plane on the ice before he turns off the propeller. The plane slides and slides for hundreds of feet, finally beginning to slow down.

But as she slows down, the plane begins to lean forward until finally it comes to a stop. The windshield faces the ground, gravity wanting to pull them down into the ice. But just before the plane leans too far, the weight brings everyone back down flat onto the landing gear. The crew crashed down in their seats, gasping for air as they were holding their breath when facing the ground.

"I swear if someone sneezed I think we would've fallen over," Elliott says, holding back his vomit.

Chuckling engulfs the plane. Then Eva urges everyone out of the plane. Oddly enough, the air feels fairly warm. Despite the amount of ice that covers this region, there isn't much cold air lingering about. The only thing that does feel cold are everyone's feet standing in the ice. It almost feels like snow, where it doesn't feel as packed. Footprints are what is left behind with each step.

Each member prepares boots that can grip the ice more easily. Once everyone is on the ice and out of the plane, Evzen asks, "What's the plan?"

"A hike first," Eva says. "We're not far from the mountains, so an hour or less of walking should be enough to get us into the region. Radek will stay with the plane. Your job is to be a quick getaway if we need it. Hover around the mountain and if you see any of us, especially Chernak, come pick us up."

"Will do, boss!" Radek salutes.

"Evzen, you lead us through that cave. You have the waypoint and you'll be our guide. If there's anything suspicious with a plant or animal, we want to hear about it," she continues.

"It'll be my pleasure," Evzen says.

"Marketa, you have your mineral detector. Whatever this treasure is, it's some kind of indestructible material. You search and be our tools, bring whatever you can carry."

"Say less," Marketa says.

Then Eva looks over at Elliott. "You and I are watching

from the front and back of the group, we keep them safe. If there's a wall we need to break through, I want Chernak there. Any gadgets or tricks you can show us, this will be the time."

Elliott nods in understanding, excited for this trip.

"Gear up. We're getting that treasure," Eva directs.

Everyone piles everything into their packs. Evzen makes sure his herbalism kit is ready, Marketa stores any tools in her pack or Chernak's saddle, Eva straps her pack in, and Elliott arms his gadgets. Radek climbs into the plane, waiting for the rest of the group to head out. Satisfied that they are ready, the Mere crew hikes out through the Burning Iceland towards Mount Spiral.

Fifteen minutes in and Evzen cannot contain himself. "I cannot wait to become the first Legendary Hunters!"

"You're really that confident," Marketa asks, nervously. "Hasn't every hunter died trying to search for treasures like this one?"

"Don't worry," Elliott says. "We're not like them. Besides, I doubt they had a sand dragon to help them. Right, buddy?"

If I wasn't with you, you probably wouldn't have made it here. Chernak huffs and puffs.

"Oh hold on. I do recall saving you several times, one of them being very recent," he refutes.

The dragon can only growl. Eva chuckles at their interaction. But then her smile dissipates when she asks, "So what are you going to do with your share of the money?"

Confused, Elliott tilts his head to the side, "What?"

"After this hunt, you'll be going back to your home and probably a picture on the wall. You'll get your share of the bet we made. What are you going to do with it?"

He forgot all about the bet. Whoever touches the treasure first has sixty percent of the money and the title of a Legendary Hunter. He forgot it! After all this time he has been feeling like a part of the group but now there's the promise they made. Now thinking about what would happen afterwards, there doesn't seem to be a clear vision of the future. What would he do with the money? Or even the title? Would he stop hunting? Would he buy a mansion like the one the crew has? But that would be pointless, he thinks. All of that money and he would hardly spend it.

Elliott opens his mouth to say something but no words come out. The only thing that he can mutter is, "I don't know."

Silence reigns over the group. Eva then opens her mouth to say something, but is interrupted by the sound of crackling. Everyone stops in their tracks and looks down to see the ice beneath them is very thin. Large cracks begin to form under their feet.

"Oh no," Evzen says. Just after he says it, the floor shatters. Everyone except Chernak falls into a steep slide of perfectly packed ice. The dragon dives into the pit to follow the rest.

The ice is unbelievably slippery and several pathways lead in various directions. Right and left, up and over, down and back, the place is like a labyrinth. The crew continues to slide down into these passageways, screaming in terror. Elliott and Eva veer left while Evzen and Marketa slide right. They do all they can to stop themselves, but the ice is too slippery. Not even their boots are enough to cause friction to stop themselves.

Towards the left, the slide makes a massive turn down and to the right. Elliott switches his scaling spikes on to drive into the ice. But it just cuts clean through, not causing much of a difference in his momentum. But it is enough for Eva to slide up and past him. He releases his grip to continue his slide but Eva comes back down, landing on top of him. He groans in pain as they continue their descent.

Marketa tries to use her grapple to stop herself from sliding, but the ice is still too slick. The grapple dangles from her belt, not grabbing onto anything. The slide leads to a chasm where there is a dropoff towards a river of molten rock. Desperately trying to make some sort of stop, it's inevitable for her to fall just over the chasm into the other side of the ice, continuing to make her descent. Her heart jumps to her throat after crossing the ravine, her soul almost leaving her body.

Evzen makes a fast fall down an ever increasing steep incline. Faster and faster he falls towards the river of flowing magma. He flails around, his legs moving sporadically until the surface holding him vanishes. The rest of his fall leads to the hot and steaming magma.

Evzen screams in horror until he is lifted into the air, his feet nearly touching the molten metal. He lifts his legs to avoid the river, heating up every inch of his body. Chernak pulls him up, following the chasm towards anyone else he can find. He manages to hear the screaming of Marketa who is spiraling down towards the river.

With one claw holding onto Evzen by the backpack, Chernak dives with the other claw to catch Marketa by the shoulder as she is sliding down the ice. Now he searches for his friend in this ravine of ice. The features in here shift from the convection beneath them. The ice lifts and falls into the magma, burning up at the touch of the metal and evaporating into the air. Each drop of ice splatters magma everywhere. Chernak dodges and swings his passengers to prevent them from getting burned.

Eva latches onto Elliott, who is still grunting in pain from the weight of another person on his stomach. The pathway tosses and turns, eventually evening out into a slight decline into a wall with sharp rocks pointing at them. Elliott turns Eva away from the spikes, shielding her from any impact.

Chernak uses his legs to grab onto the two of them. The weight of four people becomes a little tough for him. He flaps his wings as much as he can, scraping the sides of the chasm. Eventually, he brings everyone to the surface, dropping them onto the soft ice.

Everyone tumbles and the first thing they hear is Evzen laughing while he lies on his back. "Radek would've loved that," he chuckles.

Elliott laughs with him. "Is everyone alright?" he asks. The group nods a yes to him. He turns to his dragon who is lying on his stomach. "Thanks, buddy."

That adds to the times I have saved you. He seems to sigh.

Elliott helps everyone up, turning to the columns of rock ahead of them that indicate the dangerous Mount Spiral.

12

THE SPIRAL MOUNTAIN PHANTOM

The mountains are much taller up close, each one easily surpassing eight thousand feet. The slopes are so steep climbing them is near impossible, especially with the lack of cracks and crevasses. The rock is dusty but smooth like chalk with a gray color. The wind whistles around the gorges and the water below each gap of the spiral crashes against the cliffs thousands of feet below.

A narrow path of gravel and stone is what the crew takes to make their way into the mountain range. Each step is having to avoid another boulder, using both hands to climb around or above it. There is no vegetation, no sign of a tree, bush, or fern in this area. Just old rock sitting in the same place for who knows how long.

About a half an hour in squeezing through this trench for a mountain, the trail reaches the edge of the cliff where the outside of the spiral begins. The crew hugs the wall, afraid of getting too close to the edge. Down the cliff is the water from the ocean that flows into the mountains. Waves crash against the rock, making them seem dark and sparkling.

Elliott peers around the area, looking down towards the water and then up on the other side of the dropoff. The gap between him and the other cliff seems a couple miles away, no chance of jumping nor making a bridge to get across. But there is still a way to make this trip shorter, he thinks.

"Hey guys," he says from behind. "Why don't we take a shortcut by going across here," he points towards the other side of the gap.

The group looks at him with much puzzlement. "See, I want to be optimistic here, but if you think we can jump that, you're crazier than Radek," Evzen says.

Elliott gives a wry smile. "I meant Chernak can carry us two at a time to the other side. It'll minimize our trip by days."

Chernak grunts. *I can speak for myself.*

The crew, now understanding the suggestion, seems to consider it. "It'll avoid any mishaps along the way, too," Eva says.

Marketa carefully looks out towards the water. "I don't know," she says. "I don't like the idea of falling and . . . crashing and . . . drowning."

"Then you don't have to worry," Elliott says. "Instead you'll be flying and then landing . . . safely." He makes sure to add the last part of the sentence. "Just watch. Eva, if you'd care to join me," he says, extending a hand to her.

She takes it gracefully, grabs onto the saddle of Chernak, and pulls herself up with ease. Elliott joins her in the front and plants his feet in the stirrups. He tugs on the reins and the dragon jumps into the air. The breeze is harsher here. Most of the streams of wind coming from the ocean are pushed into this part of the trench. But Chernak has no problem gliding through towards the other side of the mountain range. In hardly any time at all, they make it to the other side. Looking back, Evzen and Marketa look like moving specs.

Chernak launches into the air again after dropping off Elliott and Eva to go pick up the rest. Marketa shivers just at the thought of what could happen if something were to go wrong.

"It's going to be alright, trust the fabulous beast," Evzen consoles.

"Easy for you to say," she refutes. "I'm fine with flying in my own contraption over land. This is different. I'm flying 'outside' of a bunch of metal that can at least bear some of the impact."

"Trust me, I'd rather take Chernak over Radek's absurd flying," Evzen says.

Chernak swoops in, landing perfectly in between the two of them. Evzen climbs on without hesitation. Marketa, on the other hand, is very reluctant to grab on. With some encouragement to herself, she is able to jump on behind her friend. She locks her arms around him and braces.

Evzen cheers with excitement once the dragon leaps into the air. But a tight grip around his stomach starts to hurt. Marketa hugs him, keeping her eyes closed to prevent looking down. Soon enough, Chernak lands without an impact. Her grip stays but she feels the movement of Evzen trying to get loose.

"Marketa!" he says. "Please! I'd like to breathe!"

Now opening her eyes to the sight of ground again, she lets go of her hold on him. He gasps and jumps off Chernak.

As soon as Marketa jumps off, everyone flinches at the

sound of a terrifying shriek that comes from the tops of the mountains. An enormous creature with wings comes into view, but not a bird. The wings are fuzzy with a color just like the shade of the chalky rock. It has six large legs that seem to have smaller legs on each one. The body is an ellipse and the head has two massive bug eyes with antenna protruding above them. The head and body are a black color but the wings are able to cover it from the back side.

"Nobody move," Evzen warns. "That's a shale moth. A camouflaging creature that blends in with the sides of the mountains. It's sensitive to movement and hunts its prey while hiding in plain sight."

"Good work telling us beforehand," Marketa says.

"As long as we stay out of sight and out of its range we should be fine. Hug the wall," he says.

Everyone obeys, pressing their backs against the rock. The moth lands on the tip of a mountain, gazing around for any-thing it can eat. It shrieks again before it wraps its wings around the column of stone. The skin of the wings make the creature invisible, blending in perfectly with the land.

"Now we move slowly towards the cave," Evzen says.

The crew continues with caution. Each member walks up against the walls, standing on their toes for any sign of a threat. The further they go the more they seem to be on edge. Any dust that falls from the tops of the mountains is enough to stop the group.

Another half hour flies by before they see another shale moth. It reveals itself from its camouflage searching around for any kind of movement. The crew hugs the wall again to prevent themselves from being seen.

Then Elliott feels something crawling on his finger. He jolts at the sight of a small bug with a charcoal body in the shape of a pretzel. The sides of its body are translucent wings and legs on the inner part of the body. It crawls up his arm and towards his face without making a sound. But Elliott refuses to move as it will endanger everyone else because of the shale moth.

Up and up it travels to the neck and towards his nose. Just before it could get there, Eva grabs it by the wing and tosses it quickly. It tumbles on the ground and creates a searing and crackling sound like steak on a grill.

"Sizzle beetle, nothing to worry about," she says.

"It's clear, keep moving," Evzen says, continuing to walk through the rock trail.

A few more minutes go by once they reach the other side of the range. Another dropoff is here before them in the inner spiral. The group looks over towards the center part of the spiral where multiple cave openings lead to the inside of the mountains.

"Are we ready for another ride?" Elliott suggests.

"Are you sure that's a good idea with that moth hunting us?" Marketa asks.

She's right, the moment they fly out there might be the time a shale moth will see them before they make it to the caves. On the other hand, flying fast enough to the caves will shorten the journey and avoid any other risks in this gorge.

"If we get there quick enough, we won't have to worry about the moths later, especially at night. I think it's worth the risk," Elliott insists.

The group feels hesitant, but convinced that it should be worth a try. After all, the cave is just across the chasm. If they didn't have Chernak, it would be a different story making it around the spiral.

Elliott prepares for another flight, but he feels something odd is going on. Like something is watching them. The others have the terrible sense as well, looking around for anything out of place. Then Eva sees it, a large set of legs appearing from behind wings that reaches for Elliott. Just before it can snatch him, Eva pushes him out of the way, but the legs snatch her instead.

The shale moth lifts her high in the air towards a mountaintop. Jumping back on his feet, Elliott frantically grabs onto Chernak's saddle and urges him up in the air. They chase after the moth as fast as the dragon can, flapping his wings vigorously to catch up.

The wings of the moth are so powerful it creates a booming sound with every flap. Chernak gains on the moth and Elliott reaches for Eva who is writhing. But the moth swats at them, changing directions towards another mountaintop. The dragon dodges, but the altitude is starting to become a huge toll on him. The elevation is much higher than what the plane usually travels.

Chernak gasps for air but pushes to catch up again. He uses every bit of energy to get to the monstrous beast. Bobbing and weaving around towers of stone the dragon draws closer to the moth. Just fifty feet, thirty, now ten, Elliott begins to stand up in the stirrups to reach for Eva. She reaches for him with just inches to go.

Their fingers touch when the moth swats again, striking Chernak and throwing Elliott off the saddle. His feet slip out of the stirrups and gravity begins to take him towards the ground. The force causes his body to toss and turn before he stabilizes himself in terminal velocity with his stomach facing the ground.

Chernak quickly shifts directions to save his friend at full speed, making himself look like a dart in the air. He tears through the air while Elliott tries to hover closer to him by bringing his hands closer to his thighs and pointing his toes. The ground becomes closer and closer until they seem too close for comfort. At that moment, Chernak swings beneath Elliott so he sits back into his saddle and the dragon picks them back up. They perch on top of a small mountain, about two thousand feet tall.

"We have to get to that nest before Eva becomes dinner," Elliott says, urging his friend back into the air to follow them.

The higher the moth goes, the harder it becomes to breathe. Finally, on one of the tallest parts of the mountain range, the moth lands at a nest. The nest is a hole in the rock that Eva drops inside. The area is neatly carved out but dripping with a jelly substance. Four cocoons are suspended from the ceiling that have larvae moving inside of it.

The moth flips upside down, engulfing the top with its wings, and sticks its mouth inside the nest. Four pincers reach for her but she opens her retractable spear, deflecting each one as best she can. Ducking, jumping, sidestepping, Eva does it all until she finds an opening. The pincers leave the mouth exposed, the best spot for her to plunge the point of the spear.

Blood seeps out after she backsteps away from the mouth. The moth releases an agonizing screech.

The scream of the moth can be heard for miles. Both Elliott and Chernak turn their heads towards a mountain with a distorted image. The camouflage from the moth is disrupted after moving away from something that hurt it.

"Drop me off on the back side of the nest," Elliott says. "Distract the moth and I'll get Eva."

Chernak listens, continuing to fly higher towards the opposite side of the mountain face. Once they get close enough, Elliott jumps off and releases his spiked boots. The spikes dig into the stone and grip it enough for him to climb. Quickly but carefully, he scales the mountain by keeping his body close to the wall and weighting his foot before going further. If there is even one mistake, the fall will be devastating as the rest of the mountain is a very steep angle with no ledges to hold onto.

The sand dragon circles around the moth and dives into the back with his mighty jaw. Tearing muscle and tendons, the moth shrieks again but this time comes off the mountain. The sudden shift in force flings Chernak off and is now being chased by this terrifying creature.

He takes his pursuer down to the lower parts of the mountain. Knowing that the moth is significantly bigger than he is, the best chance he has is outrunning him through the pillars of rock. He makes one sharp turn towards the right, then another to the left, but the monster does not seem deterred.

The thundering flaps of the wings only seem to be getting closer. The pincers come out to grab the dragon just a few meters away. But then, a sudden crash knocks the moth sideways. The roaring sound of a propeller grabs Chernak's attention.

"WOOOOO! Clocked you right in the face! That's three saves in two days! New record!" Radek screams from the cockpit, hoping the landing gear isn't too damaged. But now, infuriated, the moth dashes for Radek and Fiala. "Plane versus bug, baby! Let's see what you got!"

Radek pops his fingers and his neck, taking the plane towards the inner parts of the spiral. He shifts the ailerons, turns the wings, dips the plane, the only pilot they have is also the best one they know. Fiala swings around a mountain and then dives down towards the water. The moth follows, using everything to catch this annoying mechanism.

The plane pulls up, nearly hitting the water. But the moth accidentally scrapes its wing against the sides of the cliff and crashes against the water. In very little time, it recovers to return chasing the plane.

———

The breeze is more intense the higher Elliott climbs. He makes his way to the other side of the mountain, but the rock is looser than anticipated. With one step, the stone breaks apart which nearly throws him off balance. His instincts kick in to hug the wall, his heart pounds knowing that he doesn't have a safety net here. But he breathes in and out. He continues with only a few meters to go, the hole of the nest is just above his head.

Once it becomes within reach, Elliott grabs the ledge and pulls himself up with the rest of the strength he has left. He rolls into the nest and there she is, Eva holding her spear in a ready position. But she drops it at the sight of him gasping for air.

"You're crazy to climb that!" Eva says, embracing him dearly.

"I learned from the best, or the worst depending on your

point of view," Elliott says. "We need to get you out of here," he says, calling for Coil.

The pentagonal droid appears from his backpack who doesn't like the look of the place they are currently in.

"We need a cable, a long one. And I need you as an anchor," he tells him.

The robot produces a cable about sixty meters long, one that Elliott attaches to his belt and pinches the cable. He then pulls out a rope tether for Eva. A rope attached to a carabiner that he ties to create a harness for her. He wraps it around her waist and tells her to hold onto him.

"Coil, anchor just outside," Elliott says.

Coil drills himself to the side of the mountain with the cable running through him like a repel system. The two of them stand just outside of the nest with Eva's arms around Elliott's neck. He latches onto her waist to prepare for descent. He prepares another tether for himself when they get far enough down the rope so they can descend further.

Their hearts pump faster while looking down. The view is sensational, being able to see almost half the continent from here. The volcano, the Smoke Cloud, the Swamp Mountains, even the Black Desert way in the distance. Elliott then leans back on the cable and walks backwards down the mountain.

———

"There has to be something we can do!" Marketa says, trying to reach the mountain Elliott and Eva are climbing down from.

The moth continues to chase after Radek and Chernak through the mountains.

"I think I know what to do," Evzen says. "We need to get rid of that moth first. Do you have something with a high frequency?"

Marketa digs through her toolbox as quickly as she can. The first thing she finds is a frequency bar the size of her hand. "Give me a few seconds," she says.

She takes a screw bar and a small tube for a mouth piece to put together with the frequency bar. She forms a high frequency whistle that she hands to Evzen.

"Perfect!" he says. "Shale moths hate high frequencies, this should do the trick."

———

The shale moth catches up to Chernak, slamming him into the same mountain Elliott and Eva are descending from. He bites and snarls to get it off but the strength of the bug is too great. The pincers come out again to take a chunk out of Chernak. Before it does, it curls, writhes, and screeches in pain from a high pitched noise.

The moth backs off, wanting desperately to get away from this terrible noise. Its thunderous wings take it away high in the air towards its nest. The sound is so irritating it begins to climb the wall itself, knocking down rock and dust.

In no time at all, it makes its way to the nest where Elliott and Eva are still scaling down from. It doesn't see the cable nor the people, crawling over them without taking any notice of them. But the leg catches the cable, snapping it in two. The two of them fall down towards the ground. Coil breaks himself free from the anchor and dashes for them.

The little robot tries to lift his falling friends but the forces are too great. His legs are two small to carry them both. Just before they strike rock, Chernak, no longer in danger of a shale moth, swoops in to catch them. Plenty of other moths living in the area begin to fly away from the sound of a high pitched whistle.

He takes them back down towards Evzen and Marketa who are waiting patiently for their leader.

"Are you alright, Eva?" Evzen asks.

"No scratch, thanks to a certain someone," Eva says, looking towards Elliott.

The young hunter scratches the back of his head. "It was nothing. It looked like Radek showed up at a pretty good time, right buddy?" Elliott says to Chernak.

I don't know what you're talking about. I had it all under control. He snarls.

"Yeah, sure you did."

"Let's not waste any more time," Marketa says hastily. "Let's get to that cave before we see more."

They didn't waste any more time. The crew heads for the ledge again, where they can see Radek flying his plane around Mount Spiral. Chernak takes them over two at a time with complete ease. Before they know it, they have reached the center of the spiral.

The area here is darker, gloomy, and ominous. The spiral leads to a cavern opening containing sounds of echoing waves, wind, creatures, and more. Also known as the Mimicking Cavern, where the most dangerous treasures are hidden. Most treasures lying in here are leveled as Extreme, but that is only the shallow parts of the cave.

The crew stands before it, preparing for anything that comes in this last part of the journey.

"No turning back," Eva says. "If we need an extraction, I want Elliott and Chernak to grab Radek."

Elliott nods in understanding. Marketa opens her mineral detector where a green screen lights up. Evzen opens the waypoint where he prepares to lead the group.

"This is where we become Legendary Hunters," Eva says before walking in.

13

THE CAVERN OF LEGENDS

To most hunters, this cavern can be described as spine-chilling. The floor and ceiling are littered with stalagmites and stalactites. Crevasses so deep there doesn't seem to be a bottom. Bridges of brittle stone sit lying across these crevasses. Peculiar roots stick out of the walls, feeding off the water dripping from them. The light quickly diminishes from the outside, making the members of the crew turn on lanterns and flashlights. The further they walk through this cavern the bigger it seems to become. Several caves leading to different pathways sit in various spots.

Evzen leads the group with the waypoint beeping as they walk. Eva falls close behind him with her spear ready, Marketa just behind her swinging her mineral detector around the floor, and Elliott with Chernak behind them to keep watch of the back. It is so vast in this cave the footsteps echo slightly with a crunch of gravel or slap on stone.

Coil hovering right beside Elliott shakes with fear. The little robot floats closer to his master while making a low pitched zooming noise.

"It'll be alright, pal," Elliott reassures, patting him on the head.

They walk carefully over thin plates of rock across a crevasse. Each step crackles the sediments beneath them. Once across, Elliott breaks the silence again.

"So does anyone know what the treasure actually looks like?" he asks.

"Judging by the name, I'm assuming it's a large tooth," Evzen answers with some sarcasm.

Elliott sighs. "Really? I never thought about that. Is there an animal we're looking for? A fossil? An artifact?"

"Not sure," Marketa says. "Whatever it is, it's an indestructible material no one has recovered yet."

Then, as if the cave wasn't terrifying enough, a horrifying, pulsed roar echoes through the cavern. It's distant, but enough to shake everything around them, vibrating through their entire body. The group peers around with wide eyes and elevated heart rates. They eventually look at Chernak, as if hoping he was the one to make that roar.

He grunts. *Oh yeah, that was my stomach. As if I could make a roar like that.*

"Honestly, out of the many animals I have studied and learned about, I have no idea what that was," Evzen says.

Now that's more terrifying, Elliott thinks. It's bad enough that they run into several kinds of animals and have to deal with them even when Evzen knows what to do. But it's worse now that he cannot identify the roar. That means it must be an unidentified animal.

"Well, it seemed far away," Eva says. "Let's try to keep it that way."

The crew continues. Evzen takes them into a pathway that presents a marvelous part of the cavern. It seems to produce its own light from above, creating a dim yellow shade to the room. Columns form from drops of water from the ceilings.

One intriguing factor that catches Elliott's eye. Furry, winged, yellow creatures hang from the ceiling where the light emits from.

"Hey, Evzen," he says. "What are those?" Elliott asks, pointing towards the dangling creatures.

The biologist takes a look, squinting since they are so far. "Oh! Those are blaze bats!" he says. "Cute little things but can be quite dangerous. If they get startled, they scatter and the colors of their wings can cause so much disorientation it can make someone go blind."

The fascination dwindles from Elliott after hearing the last part. "Good to know," he says.

They continue through the cavern when the roar erupts again. The ground shakes again, this time slightly more vigorously. The sound turns from a roar slowly to an echoing moan. Coil hides behind Elliott this time, quivering with fear. Pebbles fall from the ceiling until the echo dissipates.

"That does not sound like it's getting any further away," Marketa says.

Evzen takes them through the cavern towards a smaller tunnel. A different sound is produced through this area. Not a roar nor a moan, but a rattling noise. High pitched rattling coming from the dark hall up ahead.

The waypoint seems to point this direction, so they continue. The rattling increases in volume as they walk inside. The light completely diminishes from the other room. Now, the only light they have are their lanterns and flashlights, which only seem to serve a limited range of vision.

The noise seems to vibrate through their bones until suddenly, it stops. Everyone now inside the tunnel feels like something is watching them. It seems too still in this area. They peer around the place and find loose gear and backpacks scattered around the floor. From the looks of it, they seem old and rusted over, broken even. Knives, pots, pans, tinderboxes, and more litter the area. What is worse is the bones from previous hunters lying here. Some separated from the rest of the bodies, others in pieces.

Then, Elliott stops at the sight of something moving close to the wall. "Guys," he says with a whisper. "Point your light up."

They obey, and their lights run across the wall and up to the ceiling. Humanoid creatures hang from the wall. They have scales for skin, thin and razor sharp claws as long as a foot, and needles sitting along their backs that rattle when they become spotted as thin as antennae. Their pointed teeth hang out of their mouths, crossed perfectly along the head horizontally. There are dozens of them.

"Run!" Elliott demands.

As soon as he says so, the humanoids drop down from the ceiling, preventing the group from going back. The only way of escape is through the rest of the dark tunnel. They circle around the group with a few attempting to drop directly on each one of them. But Chernak comes to the rescue, knocking these fiends away from them.

Elliott swiftly pulls on his wrist gadget to activate the fireworks. They pop, crackle, and sparkle on the creatures which causes them to hiss and screech. He urges his friends forward to get them out of the circle. They sprint for the other side, defending themselves as best they can. Eva uses her spear to stab and knock away any pursuers.

After being stunned, the fiends charge at them on all fours, pouncing in long strides. Their blinding speed allows them to catch up in no time at all. Just behind Elliott, one gets close enough to slash at the back of his head. He is knocked to the ground, but not by anything sharp. He turns on his back to stab the creature in the throat with his vibrating point.

Just as he gets up, he notices Coil struggling to hover back in the air. His pentagonal head has two slash marks that have cut through to the inner workings of his system, but not enough to power him down. Elliott quickly retrieves him, scooping him up to follow the rest of the group. A faint light can be seen towards the end of the tunnel, providing hope for the group.

That is, until the monsters begin to surround them again, crawling on the walls and ceiling. They begin to gather around Chernak to take him down, but he refuses to go down, shaking each one of them off before they make a slash.

Another manages to reach for Marketa by pouncing from the wall beside her. She attempts to sidestep out of the way, but the claw catches her right leg. It slices through the cloth of her pants and into the muscle where blood leaks out from. She staggers onto the ground with a yelp of pain. Eva is quick to turn to her, stabbing the humanoid in the head. She helps her up by the shoulder, practically dragging her from her feet.

Sprinting, limping, fighting their way towards the light which grows every step they take. While they grow closer towards the end, so do their assailants. The walls and ceiling seem to move with them, with every inch of rock can no longer be seen due to the amount of fiendish creatures.

As soon as it seems too late, the crew dives for the light and tumbles into the dirt below them. Almost like a barrier, the creatures stop before leaving their tunnel. The group gasps for air and the fiends crawl back into their lair.

The natural light in this part of the cavern is much brighter than the room before. Many more rock features have created columns and even boulders in peculiar shapes.

Elliott looks down at his robot, who seems to be very weak. "Coil, why did you do that?" he asks, worrisome.

Coil manages to mutter a low toned but static zoom noise, like he is saying he had to.

His master observes him and the scratches he took protecting him. His hover system and hydraulics are damaged, preventing him from flying and lessening the amount of fuel needed to function.

"Marketa, can you–" Elliott stops once he looks up to see Marketa being bandaged by Eva. Her right calf is bleeding heavily, some of the blood seeps through the first layer of bandages. She winces in pain every time Eva makes a wrap around her leg.

He and Evzen walk over to check on her. "What happened?" Evzen asks, concerned.

"What does it look like?" Marketa says, whitening her

knuckles. "One of those things cut my leg. Thanks for getting him away from me, Eva."

"Anything for you. All of you," she says. "It looks like those things hate the light. Nocturnal freaks."

"It's quite amazing, really," Evzen says. "That's another creature I've never seen. Probably for good reason, too," he says, referring to the piles of bones in the hall. "There has to be plenty of creatures here that no one has documented."

"How much further, Evzen?" Marketa asks, relieved that her leg is done being bandaged.

He holds out the waypoint, which beeps slightly faster. "We're getting closer, we should start moving."

"To a safer spot," Elliott mentions. "Marketa is hurt, that means we're hurt, too. We should find a spot to rest."

Eva likes the sound of that. She nods an agreement and offers Marketa a hand back up. She takes it, groaning to get back up while only putting minimal weight on her leg. Before they begin walking, Chernak leans beside her to offer a ride. Marketa graciously pets him on the neck. Eva helps her to push onto the saddle and put her feet in the reins. Now that they are ready, Evzen continues to lead.

"Stay cautious," Eva says to Elliott. "If anything worse happens, I want Chernak to take us out of here and find Radek."

"I promise," he says. "No need for an extraction yet. I'll be sure no one else gets hurt."

The trek continues through the never ending cavern. The trail Evzen leads them towards is declining into a small trench. The walls are moist and cold, serving more to the spine chilling feeling. The echo of footsteps lessens the further down they walk. But the noises lingering in the cave still travel to their ears. It makes each one of them wonder what else could be living down here. Even Evzen is still unable to identify them.

While being carried by Elliott, Coil alarms him with another static zoom. His screen tries to show a name but the image is blurry.

"What is it?" Elliott asks, trying to make it out.

The name of a substance is showing. The image focuses more, revealing the name of a gas. Elliott gasps, "Respirators! Now! There's toxic gas!"

No one hesitates, they all cover their mouths and search for masks. Elliott folds his mask on his face, turning on the crossed visor. The crew puts on their masks from the plane, pulling the straps over their heads.

Elliott sighs with relief that everyone has their masks on. Chernak doesn't need one since his immune system is used to the toxic fumes of the Smoke Cloud and the Black Desert in some areas.

"What kind of gas?" Eva asks.

Elliott shows what Coil is revealing from his screen. "Parasitic gas. It's invisible to the naked eye. If one breathes it in, their organs move like parasites, bubble up, and eventually . . . explode," he explains.

The group gives off a disgusted groan, even a gag from Marketa.

"And from the looks of it," Elliott continues. "There seems to be high levels of it right here."

Up ahead, the crew can see decomposing bodies from the gas. Chunks of flesh are being carried by bugs with pointed backs in sequential order. Indicating that the particular body they are looking at is fairly recent. Others are much older, where the bones are curled up in a ball and some sprawled on the ground. Their gear was also left there with more rust decaying the materials.

As they walk past the bodies, Marketa seems to look past them and admires the leftover gear they have. "Oh . . . actually . . . can we just–"

"No," Eva says. "We're here to hunt, not loot."

They walk fast through the invisible gas and past the old equipment.

"Another save from you, pal," Elliott says to Coil. "Thank you . . . for both times." His robot responds with a joyful zoom.

The ceiling grows closer to their heads and the light dims. Small caves are what they begin to walk through, still on their toes. But the sound of animals is blocked out by the noise of running water. Instead of the yellow light behind them, they see a white one lighting a small room.

Inside is an oasis, patches of grass and small shrubs grow beautifully around a pool. A spring filled by a small waterfall pouring out of the wall. The white light comes from the water that reflects off the crystals along the rock.

The crew observes the area, making sure nothing will jump out again. Coil scans the water to make sure it is clean. The spring is so pure the bottom is crystal clear, looking about ten feet deep. The bottom is covered with blue moss and algae but not a single creature in sight.

"This is a good place to stop," Eva says.

They already begin to settle in, taking off their gear and masks to release the weight. Marketa slides off Chernak after he sits down and limps towards the spring. Evzen joins her, taking some sips of the water, which happens to be the most delicious water he's ever had. He helps her to the water, giving her a cup to drink from and splashing some water on her face.

Elliott takes a seat next to Chernak, takes out a small solder and torch. He works on Coil while Eva sits just across from him.

"It's pretty lucky we found this place in the cavern," she says.

"No kidding," Elliott responds. "Given that the Mimicking Cave is probably the most dangerous place in Poclad, I'd say the chances of finding this place is near zero."

Eva agrees, nodding at the comment. She listens to the sound of the running water and the murmuring between Evzen and Marketa, indescribable from where she sits.

"Can I tell you something?" Eva asks Elliott. "And I want it to stay between us."

Elliott hesitates, wondering what she is about to say before he nods.

"Sometimes . . . I feel like coming here is a mistake," she says.

"Why do you think that?" Elliott asks, puzzled.

"You said it yourself. The chances of finding a place like this is near zero. This cavern is a place where treasure hunters go to die. We saw it back there and nearly died ourselves. I don't know what I would do if . . . if something worse were to happen to my crew. My family for that matter. I mean, we've been on plenty of adventures together, but this is different. Do you think we made a mistake?"

The concern and doubt is riddled all over her face. Elliott stops work on Coil after soldering the inside. He puts the tools down and reaches over to take her hands. "No one is going to die," he reassures. "The thing is I had some doubts before on plenty of adventures. But what I learned from each one of them is that we're never truly away from danger. Life is full of it and we can't escape it."

Eva chuckles. "Is that supposed to make me feel better?"

"Well I'm not saying to give up," he says with a nervous laugh. "But I'm saying in my experience you can overcome so much in any danger as long as you have the confidence to do so. And the skills of course but we don't need to worry about that with our group."

She laughs again, seeming to relax a bit more from his words.

"We have a couple options," he continues. "We can embrace the danger or we can wait for the danger to catch us. Embracing it sounds more fun to me."

"You sound like Radek," Eva says.

Elliott laughs. "I think I spent too much time with him."

Eva smiles and scoots closer to him, still holding onto his hands. "Thank you for coming with us. This crew loves you and they love Chernak. They've had so much fun with you both."

Coil creates a high pitched zoom sound as if asking about himself.

Eva seems to understand him. "And you of course, Coil," she giggles.

Elliott doesn't know what to say. Nothing much more can be said from what he thinks. He wants to thank her back for allowing him to join the adventure, but he doesn't know how to put it. Then the thought of the bet comes back to his mind. I don't care about that anymore, he thinks. This group has been one of the greatest things that has ever happened to him. He got to experience so much in the days that have gone by. Why give that up after? But how does he put it?

He opens his mouth to try to say something, but nothing comes out. "I . . . uh . . . I like . . . being around you all, too," he says.

Eva's smile fades slightly. That was a stupid thing to say, he thinks. She lets go of his hands and continues to lounge in the grass.

"Um . . . guys," Evzen says, staring at the waypoint.

"What is it?" Eva asks, kneeling beside him.

"Um . . . the treasure is . . . moving," he says, holding up the waypoint which is beeping faster.

Now whatever the treasure is, it is carried by some external force. Most likely an animal, possibly a stream but not likely.

"Then let's start moving," Eva says. "Are you fit to continue?" she asks Marketa.

The mechanic grunts trying to stand up. "I'm good to go," she says.

The crew gathers their gear again to begin heading back out of the room and further into the cavern. Chernak offers another ride for Marketa, who accepts again. They continue through the dark trench that leads down another tunnel. Their lights are enough to show the way. The further they go, the colder it seems to get. Some of the rock is becoming more dry, exiting past a layer of water.

As they move down, Elliott breaks the silence and the tension. "So what are all of you going to get after we find this treasure?"

"Oh!" Evzen immediately answers. "I want to get a terrarium for all of my plants! Something they can thrive in and I can walk through to take care of them."

"Can't wait to build that," Marketa says, sarcastically. "I need more parts and tools. I eventually want to make everyone a flight suit to go with the plane. That'll be something fun for everyone."

"Weren't you the one who was freaking out about crossing a chasm earlier today?" Eva teases.

Marketa's face flushes as red as her hair. "It was a long way down and there was a lot of water! I was also not in my plane. No offense, Chernak."

None taken. He grunts, but only Elliott seems to understand him.

"What about you, Elliott?" Evzen asks.

"Me?"

"Yeah, what are you going to get with the reward?"

He thinks, still unable to think about what he would get in the future. Eva asked the same question before but he still hasn't figured out an answer. The only thing he ever buys is food for him and Chernak and materials for his armor along with the gadgets. Nothing else comes to mind. "I'm not sure," is all he can say again.

The end of the path sheds an orange light coming from the other side. As soon as they see it appear, the roar comes again. This time it is significantly louder, pounding the eardrums. It shakes the tunnel, so much so it begins to crack and collapse. The team dashes forward towards the light before it caves in. The falling rocks quickly turn to falling boulders. They follow the incline, dodging debris as much as they can.

Without a scratch, the crew manages to slip by into a new part of the cavern. The tunnel is now a plugged hole in the wall after the dust clears. This is the most open area they've come across. The entire place is like one big field of rock with a ravine cutting across the middle. The incline they stand on runs down towards the field and then leads to the ravine. The orange light seeps through the ceiling, giving more of an amber color than orange.

Evzen holds the waypoint, beeping faster now. "It's here!" he says.

"Alright! Time to search!" Eva says, her heart racing just thinking about this treasure.

Marketa drops down from Chernak on her good leg, waving her mineral detector around for anything remotely close to the material they are looking for. Elliott rushes with Evzen to look for the treasure in the field area. The other side of the cavern is blocked off by the ravine, which makes them look in the area they stand in first.

Each one of them dust off sand and gravel for anything peculiar. Some crystals are stuck in the stone but nothing of the value they are currently looking for. Gems of great rarity are implanted in the walls but nothing that is impenetrable. Fossils of creatures that haven't been seen for thousands of years are still embedded in the ground, but even the tooth fossils fit nothing of what they are looking for.

Coil scans for each stone Elliott picks up but each one is declined by two zipping noises. Marketa scans each mineral Eva stumbles upon but still nothing. Evzen follows the waypoint, hovering it in the air and the ground to see if it changes. He nearly falls over the edge of the ravine just looking at it. He peers down into the crevasse, which isn't as deep as he thought. Forty feet is what he is estimating.

"Have any of you found anything?" Elliott asks.

"Not yet," Evzen says. "But we might be able to find something down there." He points down into the crack in the ground.

The rest of them rush over to observe the natural features. "I know for damn sure I'm not climbing down that," Marketa says. "But take the mineral detector if you are." She hands the device to Elliott without reluctance.

He takes it and sets it down to retrieve an item from his backpack. Since the cable from Coil has severed from the shale moth, he takes out a thin cord of rope tied neatly.

"How's your grip strength, Evzen?" Elliott asks, preparing an anchor system.

The cartographer looks at his hands. "I mean . . . my hands get sweaty," he says nervously.

"Well then I'll need them to not be, we're going down there with this," Elliott ties the rope around stakes to create a knot that looks like a figure eight. He leans on the rope and begins to walk down the wall of the ravine. He scales down with ease, landing on the ground below safely. "Your turn," he yells.

Evzen wipes his hands on his thighs and takes some dirt to cover his palms. He pulls on the rope to test and then climbs down. Struggling and shaking, he manages to reach the bottom without fail.

Now that the two of them are here, Elliott waves the detector around. Many more minerals scattered around the walls are of much more rarity. One in particular cannot be identified, a light brown rock. He takes a small pickaxe from his pack and picks at the stone around it.

"What about this?" he asks, the stone more apparent. The material is smooth and velvety.

Evzen waves the waypoint around it but starts shaking his head. "No, that's not what we are looking for. Plus it isn't moving so I assume it has to be somewhere else."

The walls shake again, the roar intensifies which seems closer to them than ever. The vibrations run through their flesh and bones, their organs shake inside them. It stops suddenly, causing the two of them to look quicker before whatever is making the noise comes closer.

"Is there anything that you can think of that might make that noise?" Elliott asks.

Evzen thinks. "Nothing that has been proven. There are creatures of myth like the one monster that created the Devouring Canyon."

"But that's miles from here," Elliott refutes.

"It's still possible," Evzen says. "The monster is said to roam the underground, creating vast tunnels with its enormous jaws throughout the continent. But that's just stories I read."

"Yeah . . . I hope that's only just in stories," Elliott says. Coil shudders a bit in his hand.

"Have you seen anything?" Eva asks from above.

"Not yet," Elliott responds, but stops looking when the rock shakes yet again.

The two of them stand still at the sound of something moving on the other side of the wall down where the ravine ends. Evzen looks at the waypoint, which is beeping faster than ever. The two hunters look at each other with both astonishment and a bit of panic.

Suddenly, the walls at the end of the ravine crumple and explode, sending huge amounts of debris in multiple areas. A gargantuan monster bursts through the walls. Its pointed, razor sharp teeth are as large as small vehicles and glowing a bright teal color. The skin of this beast is like granite and bedrock that seems rigid. Its roar deafens their ears but does not stop its movement.

Elliott and Evzen run for their lives. Each step of this creature rumbles everything around it, crushing boulders and dirt below. It swings its head around in a blind movement, not knowing what is around the vicinity. That is until he brings down its head into the ravine, slicing through the rock like paper. The two victims race past the rope, knowing that there is no time to climb.

Closer and closer the creature comes, the rumbling is enough to lift them off the ground for a second. The forces accumulate, making the two of them fall over. The beast roars again, so close the hunters have to cover their ears to avoid internal damage. It stops its movement and slams its head down, just inches from Elliott and Evzen. Dirt and dust shoots in the air from the massive impact of the creature lying motionless on the floor.

Elliott makes sure his partner is alright in which Evzen nods yes while still admiring the beast.

Hearts pounding, adrenaline rushing, lungs gasping, the two of them slowly stand back up. "What happened?" Elliott asks. "Did you guys do something?" he yells from below.

"Not a thing, thanks for making sure we're alright," Eva says.

"Likewise," he says.

Evzen walks closer to the creature. Elliott tries to stop him to ensure the creature doesn't eat him if it moves. But the biologist listens, feels around the rough skin, all with a jaw dropping expression.

He looks up at Elliott and says, "It's . . . it's dead."

"What do you mean? That's not possible! There's not a sign of injury!" Elliott says, feeling around the body and teeth that continue to glow.

"It is if it reaches its lifespan limit," he says. "If it's been living here for as long as I think it has, then it has to have reached the limit now."

While observing the body of this ancient creature, Elliott can't help but notice a tear falling from Evzen's eye. A creature this beautiful and this old is something to be appreciated. It is truly something worth observing.

He waves the waypoint and the screen shows one word that says 'Found' while putting around the teeth. "G–guys! We found it!" he says, now letting the tears fall from his face.

The crew cheers with the most joy they have been in the entire adventure. Chernak roars in triumph, Eva hugs Marketa, Elliott and Evzen jump up and down while embracing each other. The excitement fills their entire soul, they can feel their hearts pumping in their throats.

Evzen's smile fades after their embrace while he looks at the teeth. "I don't know how I feel about taking a part of it," he says. "This creature is sacred."

Elliott's excitement turns to sympathy. "It's part of the job," he says. "Do you want to say a few words?"

The bald hunter's lips quiver just thinking about it, but nods. He takes a deep breath before speaking. "Oh great and wonderful beast," he begins. "I wish we could have met you before your passing. We will forever hold a memory of you and we thank you. We hope your memory will bring great wealth to our crew, physically and emotionally."

Satisfied that his words sunk in, Evzen gestures for Elliott to begin the extraction process of the tooth. He uses his pick to dig under the gums of the front bottom tooth that have seemed to decay over time. He wiggles it around to try and get it loose and no matter how hard he pulls on the pick there doesn't seem to be a scratch on the tooth.

"I might need some help," Elliott stresses.

Evzen comes over to help pull on the tooth. They wiggle and twist, wiggle and twist, the tooth starts to come loose. They pull with all of their might until it pops off, causing the two of them to fall onto their back.

"We got it!" Elliott screams.

Eva and Marketa cheer while they hold onto Chernak. Elliott takes off his pack and sets it on the ground. There are straps attached to the side of it that are barely visible. He pulls on them to strap the tooth onto the pack so as to carry it out while also putting Coil on the top of his pack. The tooth is heavy, but lighter than he thought.

"Alright, let's get out of here, shall we?" Elliott tells Evzen.

They climb around the magnificent beast when the cavern starts to rumble. A roar is not what caused it, but it doesn't appear to stop. It grows in intensity with sand and dirt beginning to flood the area.

"Serpent's crystals," Elliott curses. "Move! We have to get out of here!"

The two of them scramble to get out of the ravine. The weight of the tooth greatly impacts Elliott's climbing ability, but he still manages to make it out. Evzen gets up first, helping Elliott onto his feet. The group heads for the blocked exit but the entire room is filling up with sediments quickly. They slip and slide, not being able to hoist themselves up as if they are in a current.

"Chernak! Get out of here!" Elliott says.

No! He seems to say, writhing in the sand.

"Go now! Get Radek! Make an entryway for him! Go!" he demands.

The dragon hesitates but listens to his master with as much speed as he can muster. He travels to the top of the cavern, bursting through the ceiling until he cannot be seen.

Most of the sand comes through the way they came in. It fills up like an hourglass, the ravine is now entirely filled. The crew tries to stick together and keep their heads up at the same time. As much as they fight the incoming earth, nothing seems to be enough to break through. Marketa tries to use her grapple but it has nothing to grasp onto.

There doesn't seem to be a way out. Nothing at all. Eva reaches for the hands of everyone in the crew, including Elliott. They come together, scared, desperate, and sad. Elliott does everything he can to get them to a safer spot, but nothing helps. The dirt just begins to cover each one of them, preventing any sort of escape. He can only look into the faces of his new friends, worried that Chernak might not make it.

The sediments are reaching their necks. They keep their hands out of the dirt but it doesn't seem like it will matter anytime soon. It seems like only seconds before they become completely covered.

In that moment just before giving up, the sound of a propeller makes its way into the cavern. First a dragon and then a plane comes out of a large hole in the ceiling that quickly starts to crumple. A ladder drops from the bottom of the plane.

Chernak glides over to pick up his team. One person for each limb, he picks them up with all his strength from the loose dirt.

They burst out and he soars by the ladder for Evzen and Marketa to grab hold of. Elliott and Eva climb onto the saddle, watching the other two being hoisted up into the plane.

With the ladder on a mechanical pulley system, Marketa and Evzen rise into the fuselage to hear the sound of the crazy pilot they know and love. "Finally I get some action!" he says, following Chernak. As soon as he looks at the creature below he yells, "What is that?"

"Pay attention!" Evzen screams as they almost strike a stalactite.

There is still an opening that the massive beast created in the wall. Elliott guides Chernak through and Radek follows close behind. The cavern they enter is still collapsing from the amount of digging made by the monster. Boulders and debris fall, making Chernak bob and weave through the air. What's worse is the lava below them that the rocks fall into, making the molten materials shoot up.

Up, down, right, left, up and over, around, Chernak and Radek focus all of their energy to make tight turns around all of these objects. Radek, not having to use this much energy on the plane before, is pulling and turning with all of his force. His passengers struggle to hold onto something, trying to get themselves buckled.

A group of blaze bats scatter the ceiling, in which Elliott tells Eva and Chernak to close their eyes. Radek nearly looks directly at them.

"Oh wow! That was bright!" he says, squinting his eyes.

After opening their eyes, Chernak almost faceplants into the ground but pulls up in time. The debris doesn't seem to stop, a large chunk of the cave falls over that almost blocks their path. They dodge out of the way, still trying to prevent themselves from getting hit.

Fiala is taking some damage. Chernak is agile and able to pass without a trace. The plane is still having to take hit after hit, creating dents in the fuselage and wings. Radek tries his best to avoid the biggest problems. He scrapes through narrow paths, creating sparks from the impact.

A bright light shows at the end of the cave that the plane goes for. It is quite narrow. Radek steadies the plane, leads it up at an incline, the top scrapes against the ceiling and the landing gear skids on the bottom. With just the right fit, Fiala squeezes through up and out of Mount Spiral before Chernak, somehow passing them in the chaos.

Chernak flies through as best as he can. A large part of the mountain blocks the exit. Elliott tells Eva to duck so that his dragon can plow through the stone. They, too, make it out of Mount Spiral, following just behind the plane.

"We did it!" Elliott screams, raising his fists in the air.

Everyone from the plane cheers triumphantly, laughing hysterically from the chaotic adventure. Elliott and Eva, unbelievably relieved, turn to each other smiling. Eva, with no hesitation at all, pulls him in for a kiss on the lips. His eyebrows rise afterwards and his smile widens.

"We did it, alright," he says, his face blushing.

THE BIRTH OF LEGENDARY HUNTERS

Chernak soars up to the beaten and battered plane close enough for Eva and Elliott to walk into the fuselage door to meet the rest of the crew still cheering their hearts out.

"How is everyone feeling?" Eva asks.

"Better than ever!" Radek yells. "Let's do it again!"

Everyone denies it, half knowing Radek would probably turn the plane around to literally do it again. Eva checks on Marketa's wound, which she nearly forgot about after the entire event.

"So how was it? Was it dangerous enough for me?" Radek asks.

"More than dangerous!" Elliott says. "It was amazing. You would've loved it."

"Oh, I bet!" he admits.

"There were so many animals down there!" Evzen mentions. "What are we going to call that large beast?"

Everyone grows silent for a second when Elliott suggests, "What about the Tunnel Carver?"

The crew seems to agree with the name, nodding their heads in agreement.

"Oh what about those rattlers? Can we call them Pitch Rattlers?" Evzen asks excitedly.

"Damn rattlers got my legs!" Marketa says angrily.

"Battle scars! I love it! Now you have a story, Marketa!" Radek says from the cockpit.

Elliott takes the glowing teal tooth off his backpack, admiring its beauty. We actually did it, he thinks. Everything that he has worked up to leads to this moment. They are truly the first ones to retrieve a Legendary treasure.

"What do you think will happen once we get back to the Hub?" Evzen asks.

"I imagine a big celebration," Elliott says. "I know a place to eat."

"That reminds me," Radek says. "Are we going to Studeny Brazina or are we going straight back to the Hub?"

Eva reads the room, looking at the completely dirty and exhausted crew. "Can you make it all the way back?"

"Sure can! You all just sit back, relax, and enjoy the ride back home."

"And this is an actual relaxation?" Marketa asks, ensuring he won't do anything crazy.

"I promise this time," he says.

Elliott glances at Eva, who locks eyes with him. "I told you it would be alright," he says. "I'll meet you guys there, I'm going to fly with Chernak for a while."

He opens the door to beckon Chernak towards the plane

to pick him up. He hops on comfortably and soars just behind them.

They fly past the Burning Iceland and Studeny Brazina with ease. The passengers of the plane fall sound asleep in this smooth ride. Elliott can't help but think about what he should say once they get back.

He grunts. "What do I do, buddy? What should I say once we get back?"

Say you want to join. I know I do. He seems to say.

"You think we should stay with them, too? In the mansion and all?"

Would I still get my own bed?

"No, the bed would be gone and you'd live outside. Of course you will get your own bed," he says, slightly annoyed.

Sounds like a lot of work.

"You are a lot of work, but you don't see me complaining."

The dragon growls.

"I would take it back if it wasn't true. But the point is we would've been able to make it that far without them. I can't . . . I wouldn't know what to do afterwards. What do you think?"

I think that as long as I get a ton of treats I'll be fine wherever you go.

<hr>

After hours of flying, the plane manages to make it back to Rosbocovac. The runway opens for them and Radek lands the plane haphazardly from the damaged landing gear. But the clamp catches and they descend back into the dome of the Mere

Mansion. Elliott and Chernak land just outside the entrance, waiting to turn in their treasure.

No one takes any time to wash or change, they bring the Colossal Tooth out of the mansion and begin heading towards the Bank. The people in the streets cannot help but stare at the wonderful treasure they have in their possession. All activity seems to stop as they walk closer to the temple-like building. Cooking, dancing, gambling, they all stop to follow the crew into the hub of the waypoints.

"We are going to be the most famous hunters in history," Elliott mentions to Eva.

She chuckles. "But you're the one who touched it first. You'll get all the fame."

"Actually," he says, looking her in the eyes while they walk. "I was thinking . . . I'd like to join your crew, along with Chernak and Coil. If that's alright?"

Eva lets a big smile loose across her face. She walks closer to him, holding him by the arm. "It took you long enough to ask. I would like that very much," she says, leaning her head on his shoulder.

Then another thought comes to mind. "Oh and uh–"

As if reading his mind she cuts him off. "Yes you can take me out," she laughs.

They walk into the Bank, everyone inside grows silent as they walk in. They gather around them and make a walkway for them towards the front desk. Bohdan stands there, jaw dropping at the sight of Elliott and the crew.

Once they head to the desk, everyone stands still. "My friend," Bohdan says. "Is that . . . is it truly . . . "

Before he can finish his question, Evzen hands the waypoint

to the owner and Radek lifts the tooth in the air. "WE ARE LEGENDARY HUNTERS!" he screams at the top of his lungs.

Every person inside the Bank cheers, holding up their hands, clapping, and jumping. The workers throw their hats in the air, confetti flies from people's hands, drinks spill across the floors. The closest people around them immediately ask questions about their travels, handshakes, and even autographs. Bohdan, who is also celebrating, calls for wagons of I's and for a place for the Colossal Tooth to be framed.

"So," Eva says to Elliott. "What are you doing with your share of the money?"

He looks up at the crew, who is having the time of their lives being congratulated by all these people. He watches them being given gifts, necklaces, and signing shirts.

He looks back at Eva and says, "I'll give it to them. I don't need it. I have all the treasure I need right here." He then pulls her by the waist, gently presses his hand on her cheek and jaw, and leans in for a kiss. She wraps her arms around his head as she kisses him back. Everyone around them cheers even louder as they watch the scene.

EPILOGUE

The city of Rosbocovac holds a massive celebration. Fireworks go off, the crew gets a picture of them with the tooth and framed on the most apparent place on the wall inside the Bank. Elliott gets recognized officially as the youngest treasure hunter to have seventeen extreme treasures in his book. Everywhere they go, they get recognized and people ask for anything remotely close to an autograph.

After a long day, the team is brought to Zuzana's restaurant, who has been getting more service than ever before. They sit at a bench while stuffing their faces with the delectable food.

"This is amazing!" Radek says, peeling the meat off a serpent. "Best food I ever had."

"You always say that," Marketa says.

"But this time I mean it! How can something smell so bad but tastes so good," he says, referring to the sap.

"I'm glad you like it, my little sap," Zuzana says, glad that she can provide food for them. "And that was very generous of you, Elliott, you didn't need to give me such a big donation."

"It was nothing, Zuzana. I love your food and your affection. You deserve it," he says.

"Can you adopt me?" Radek says.

"Ignore him," Eva says, munching on her scorobeetles.

"So what should we do next?" Evzen asks. "We've got the first Legendary treasure. Should we go for another?"

"Not for a while," Eva says. "We need to rest, for a long time."

"But now everyone is going to try and find the others," Marketa says. "What will we do for another adventure?"

Everyone seems to look at Elliott for that suggestion. He thinks and pulls out one of Evzen's maps of Poclad. He stares at it and points to the middle of the continent. "No one has figured out the Soundless Plains yet," he says.

"Alright!" Radek screams. "A place where I can go more crazy! I'm ready!"

The crew laughs and nod in agreement with the idea. They finish their food and prepare for a long rest at home.

ABOUT THE AUTHOR

EZEKIEL ELIZALDE was born in Austin, Texas and raised in the suburbs. I was shown vast amounts of stories through movies, TV shows, books, and games growing up. Most of them being an adventure based genre, allowing me to spur my imaginative mind. Some of those stories are written by my favorite authors such as Jules Verne, C.S. Lewis, and John Flanagan. Inspiration is everything to me and I want to share that feeling with the rest of the audience through an adventure that everyone can jump into. A new world that someone can look away from reality every once and a while, possibly gaining an idea to put into the real world to make it a better place.